I0657537

NO JOBS
AVAILABLE

NO JOBS
AVAILABLE

**A LAID-OFF WHITE-COLLAR WORKER CHASES
THE LOST AMERICAN DREAM**

A Novel of Business and Crime and Love Lost

Zane Smith

ABSOLUTELY AMAZING eBOOKS

Published by Whiz Bang LLC, 926 Truman Avenue, Key West, Florida 33040, USA.

No Jobs Available copyright © 2017 by Zane Smith. Electronic compilation/ paperback edition copyright © 2017 by Whiz Bang LLC.

All rights reserved. No part of this book may be reproduced, scanned, or transmitted in any form or by any means, electronic or mechanical, including photocopying, recording, or any information storage and retrieval system, without permission in writing from the publisher. Please do not participate in or encourage piracy of copyrighted materials in violation of the author's rights. Purchase only authorized ebook editions.

This is a work of fiction. Names, characters, places, and incidents either are the product of the author's imagination or are used fictitiously, and any resemblance to actual persons, living or dead, businesses, companies, events, or locales is entirely coincidental. While the author has made every effort to provide accurate information at the time of publication, neither the publisher nor the author assumes any responsibility for errors, or for changes that occur after publication. Further, the publisher does not have any control over and does not assume any responsibility for author or third-party websites or their contents. How the ebook displays on a given reader is beyond the publisher's control.

For information contact:
Publisher@AbsolutelyAmazingEbooks.com

ISBN-13: 978-1945772634 (Absolutely AmazIng Ebooks)
ISBN-10: 1945772638

An *unemployed* existence is a worse negation of life than death itself.
                                        - Jose Ortega y Gasset

Without work all life goes rotten.
                                        - Albert Camus

Must the hunger become anger and the anger fury before anything will be done?
                                        - John Steinbeck

To my daughter Anne who is always
there when I need her.

NO JOBS
AVAILABLE

ONE

I knew immediately that something was wrong. It was really out of character for Freddie to ask his secretary, Malvina, to phone and set up a meeting. Way out of character. In the nine years I worked for him as a corporate purchasing agent, he never, repeat never, used Malvina to schedule meetings with his direct reports. He much preferred to drop by our offices and tell us in person, all three of us: Donna, Charley and me.

"Come on up to my digs at 2:30 p.m.," he'd say. "We'll have a cup of coffee, talk about the Frazier account." That kind of thing. Or, if he was in a rush, he'd telephone himself.

But he never filtered his messages through Malvina. Claimed personal contact was the most democratic way to work with employees. And Freddie was always mindful of how he treated people. He used a stream of platitudes to instruct Donna, Charley and me, all of them kind of corny and shopworn but well meant. Regarding the democratic way to do things, he liked to say, "You never know if the little guy you stepped on while you're busy clawing your way up the ladder will find some way to strip the rungs and keep you from reaching the top. There's a lesson in that, my friends. Be just as nice to the lady who cleans your desks every night as you are to me."

With that he'd tilt back in his soft leather

executive chair and chuckle, the muted light from the Stiffel floor lamp behind his left shoulder bouncing off his wrinkled bald dome. The rest of us, clustered around his desk, would sort of smile and laugh in a subdued manner. Then, as if on key, one of us would invariably say, "Who you kidding? You treat us like dog shit." That would break everybody up of course, including Freddie, and we'd all erupt in belly laughs.

A lot of that humor had been missing the last few months in the tense atmosphere of takeover rumors. In July, the Wall Street Journal reported that Shaley International, our chief competitor and industry leader in the field of kitchen and bathroom hardware, had initiated talks to buy our company, Bowkart Industries, USA. A terrifying notion for white-collar employees at the corporate staff level like myself, the most vulnerable of all in a takeover. That's because in a merger the acquiring company decides what functions stay and what functions go, and overhead staff functions are always the first to go. To put it in plain words: Many Bowkart employees soon would be out on the street, out of work and shit out of luck, while Shaley International employees would remain eating high off the hog.

To aggravate matters, this was the worst possible time to be job hunting. The country's "real" unemployment rate had steadily increased the past several years and now stood nationally at an unprecedented 10.8 percent, its highest level since the Great Depression of the thirties. I say "real" because the government claimed an unemployment rate of 5.5 percent, a number that made the current administration look good, but did not include the millions who just gave up looking for work and relied on welfare to subsist. Political deceit at the highest level of government, practiced by both Democrats and Republicans, the only difference being that Democrats were more adroit at manipulating the unemployment numbers and fooling the public.

Unfortunately, the unemployment rate was climbing, its devastating effect, in particular, falling across the shoulders of white-collar workers. Americans fought with illegal Mexican workers for low-paying jobs at Walmart and Burger King. Tent cities of homeless people, unemployed and desperate and hungry, dotted the American landscape. That kind of bad.

Sure, the stock market was booming. Hell, it should be, given the lavish tax breaks handed over to corporations by a too-friendly Congress and Administration. Of course, you never get something for nothing. There's the ubiquitous quid pro quo of private companies greasing the palms of greedy politicians to vote on issues in their favor.

Anyway, I was understandably fidgety that Friday afternoon at 2:30 p.m. as I rode the elevator to the twelfth floor of the Bowkart Industries, USA building in downtown Atlanta. The elevator's bland and soothing background music didn't work. My stomach was as twisted as a snake coiled for attack. It was September 30, end of the fiscal quarter, the time when Ebenezer Scrooge executives decide to cut costs for the upcoming quarter. Meaning hapless employees like yours truly. And I was in no position to survive a layoff.

I took a few deep breaths and walked into Freddie's outer office and was not surprised to see Donna and Charley, pacing the anteroom in front of Malvina's desk. When I raised my eyebrows at them, they shrugged their shoulders. The taut set of Charley's mouth told me he was angry while Donna's eyes radiated fright. She was a forty-eight-year-old single mother with two teenagers to support, a big mortgage on her Buckhead condo and a jerk-off boyfriend who was out of work most of the time and sponging off her.

"Hey," I said with a fake smile plastered across my face, "it can't be that bad. Right, Malvina? Your good buddy Sam O'Hara says so."

"Yeah, right, Sam," she answered while studiously avoiding my eyes. Not a good sign. Malvina started working for Freddie shortly after I did, and I knew her well enough to interpret her signals. She leaned over her desk and frowned at a report she was making pencil notes on, behaving as if Charley, Donna and I weren't in the room. Normally, she'd banter back and forth with us. The lady was like her boss that way. She enjoyed teasing us and could handle it when we teased her right back. Yeah, one great big happy family.

Not today. With the strained look on her face, Malvina showed all of her fifty-eight years, every damn one of them, as if each weighed a ton and was slowly grinding her into the thinly carpeted floor of the office.

The intercom on her desk buzzed and startled us. Charley and Donna whirled around and my head snapped up. We were all on edge.

Malvina flipped the switch. "Yes sir?"

"They out there?" I heard Freddie's disembodied voice float through the speaker. It sounded dispirited, gloomy.

"Yes sir."

"Send 'em in."

Malvina flipped the switch and nodded at us. We opened the door to Freddie's office and marched inside single file, like mourners at a funeral procession.

"Sit down," he said, waving us to three seats obviously prearranged in front of his desk.

Freddie Walsh, behind his oversize desk, looked like a puppy trapped in a lion's cage. He was in his early fifties, stood 5'4" and weighed, as he liked to tell us, "as much as a bantam rooster soaked in bourbon." The large executive desk and chair just about swallowed him. When he was in a joking mood, which was most of the time, he'd often stand side by side with me, my 6'1" frame towering over his 5'4", making him look dwarf-like by comparison. He'd tug my sleeve and say in a falsetto voice, "Take me to the movies, Daddy." A real kidder and a mighty fine boss. The sweetest guy I ever worked for in my entire career, all thirty years of it, plus four years in the Marine Corp. Donna, Charley and I loved him.

Not that everybody in the company agreed with us about Freddie. Some top executives laughed at him behind his back, the big joke being that he wasn't the brightest bulb in the marquee. They speculated how company executives put up with a guy who "looked like a cue ball and was just as dense as one." Well, screw them. I'd take Freddie any day of the week, particularly compared to some of those know-it-all Gen X cutthroats and Millennial wise-asses I'd seen populating Bowkart's executive hallways. Their nasty criticisms obscured the fact that Freddie was street smart and wise to the ways of corporate politics. Otherwise he never could have survived thirty years with Bowkart and made it to the top of his profession as Corporate Director of Purchasing.

Now he was leaning back in his executive chair, his head sunk on his chest, hands gripping the arm rests so hard the leather creaked. Not the tiniest hint of a smile cracking his features. He looked less like my old friend and the corporate purchasing director for Bowkart Industries, USA than a despairing papa about to tell his adoring children their mother died in a plane crash.

He really cared for us, Donna and Charley and me. Unlike most bosses who didn't give a shit about their subordinates but try to hide it behind phony smiles and pats on the back, Freddie genuinely wanted us to succeed and enjoy our work and our private lives. On one occasion, he loaned Donna $5,000 so she could make the down payment on her new Buick. In another instance, Freddie made sure I received full pay for the six weeks I missed from work, that God-awful time when my teenage daughter Cindy was killed, when I tried to drown myself in a truckload of scotch. He stood by me through that terrible period, a boss and a friend who cared.

Donna, Charley and I were close to Freddie, for

many years his only family. Freddie, a widower for twelve years now, didn't have children. His entire existence was work, work, work. Reminded me of Wolf Blitzer at CNN, who never seemed to go home. For Freddie, this schedule was typical: fifteen hours a day, six days a week, leaving Sunday open for tending to his ailing mother in a nursing home high in the North Georgia mountains.

Freddie sighed and glanced at each of us in turn. His eyes radiated sorrow, compassion. "I'm afraid I'm the bearer of bad news."

Crushing words. I had instinctively known it was coming, had felt it in my bones, but at that moment it hit home with a devastating finality. I was being canned. I clasped my hands together and leaned forward in my chair, in silent prayer. The last time I kneeled before the good Lord and asked him for anything was after the worst catastrophe of my life. Six years ago, and still as bone-chilling fresh in my mind as if it happened yesterday. When my sixteen-year-old daughter, Cindy, was killed, after her Toyota Camry spun-off a tire and crashed on I-85 just north of downtown Atlanta.

"What's up, boss?" Charley asked in his usual booming bass voice. Acting as if he didn't know. Of the three of us, Charley was in the best position to weather a storm. He was single and lived frugally in an inexpensive apartment complex south of Atlanta, close to Hartsfield Airport.

Donna, Charley and I had great jobs. We flew regularly to Bowkart's eleven plants scattered across the USA, Canada and Mexico, to resolve vendor-related problems and help plant managers implement corporate purchasing policies. Except for the inordinate amount of travel, a good life, without the pressures that plant employees confront daily, and with all the hefty corporate benefits.

Until now.

"I don't have to tell you about the rumors," Freddie said. "You've all heard them. About Shaley International taking over our company ... Well, it's true." He leaned forward across his desk and clasped his hands. His face went through a dozen contortions. "You're all going to be laid-off."

Despite knowing this was coming, I gasped. So did Donna. Charley sat there, stone-faced, his jaw muscles rippling. It was one thing to know the ax would fall. It was another thing to feel its cold blade slice through the back of your neck.

"How much time do we have left?" Donna asked in an unsteady voice.

Freddie placed his elbows on the desk and rested his face in his hands.

"That bad, uh?" Charley said.

Freddie nodded. "That bad."

"C'mon, Freddie," I said. "When?" My hands felt cold and damp.

"Effective immediately," he replied, and jumped up from his chair. "God, forgive me. How I hate telling you this."

It was probably a calculated move to ease our moment of pain. Freddie, ever the considerate manager, was trying to divert attention from our own problems by focusing on his outburst and apparent discomfort. Or, perhaps, it was his attempt to shake off the crushing guilt he felt at facing us with this terrible news.

I remembered him telling me once that even the most shocking news subsides to dry, objective facts over time. So, if you're getting bad news, stop thinking about it and do something else until the emotion has drained from the issue. Then return to it, but only then. Good advice.

Advice I couldn't follow right now, no matter how hard I tried. Not many companies were going to hire a fifty-one-year-old with narrow experience, particularly one without a college degree. I felt as if the entire corporate building was collapsing, brick by brick, on my head.

"Oh, my God," Donna said and started weeping silently. Tears rolled down her cheeks in tiny parallel streams.

"How about severance?" Charley asked.

Freddie Adam's apple bobbed up and down. "You and Donna get two months. Sam, because he's been here longer, gets three months."

"That's all?" I said. "You've got to be kidding me."

"I'm not. Sorry," Freddie muttered.

"But I've been here nine years," I said. "Three months is ... hell, nothing." I spread my hands, pleading for Freddie's support.

He didn't answer. Probably couldn't.

"Insurance?" Charley asked through gritted teeth.

"One month for each of you, then you're on your own."

"That sucks," Charley spat out.

Freddie cringed. "Look, I went to bat for you, for all three of you. The executives upstairs told me you're lucky to get anything at all. They're not legally bound to give you a red cent. That's their right. So be thankful for what you got."

"Oh, how gracious of them," Charley snarled. "Fact is, they don't give a rat's ass about common everyday employees like us."

"Look, we're all taking a beating," Freddie pleaded.

"Yeah," Charley said, "We know. Just ask our bank accounts."

"Believe me, I did what I could, but the guys on the top floor wouldn't budge. At least you'll be able to file for unemployment."

"Big deal," Charley grumbled. "Three-hundred a week for six months. Won't hardly pay my rent."

Freddie winced and slinked down in his chair.

"The top floor guys," I said, "could have given us a better severance package if they wanted to."

"Yeah," Freddie replied, "they could have, but they didn't. Not when they're laying off three thousand employees today across the board. They can't play favorites."

"Oh, my God, my God," Donna mumbled to herself, her hands pressed to her face.

"Listen," Freddie said, "I'm not making excuses for them. They're only doing what every other company across the country is doing now that it's belt-tightening time. Handing out as little as possible because profit margins have hit the floor. You all know how bad the economy is. I don't like it any more than you do. But that's the way of corporate life today. As unpleasant as it is."

"Shit," I said, the implication of Freddie's words just sinking in. I was diabetic, had been for thirteen years. My average cost of insulin, syringes, glucose testing supplies, doctor's visits and related medications ran about a grand every month. Another expense I'd now be forced to absorb. As a diabetic, I'd have trouble buying a decent insurance policy. Nothing I could afford, anyway. Health insurers were cutting back and restricting coverage, and insurance costs had skyrocketed as a result. As it was, Donna, Charley and I paid six-hundred bucks a month each for minimum coverage. The outrageous cost of protection left working stiffs like us sucking hind tit, our only option to pray for good health.

"How about you, Freddie?" Charley asked. "What happens to you?"

A shadow of guilt slid across Freddie's face. "I'm okay. I may have to go back to the local Atlanta plant as purchasing manager, but I'll still be on the payroll ... I think."

Donna struggled to gain control of herself. She wiped her eyes with a lacy handkerchief. "Do we work our notice?"

"Sorry," Freddie replied, his voice subdued. "Today is it."

"Today?" I asked, stunned.

"Today." Freddie stared at the pencils and pens on his desk as if they were the most fascinating objects in the world. "By 5:00 p.m."

And that was it. Oh yeah, we sat around for a

while in Freddie's office and commiserated with one another until the shock wore off. All the time Freddie sweating and squirming, embarrassed and heartbroken by having to let us go. I felt bad for him and worse for myself. Finally, we headed back to our offices and packed our belongings and left.

I never saw Freddie or Donna or Charley again. Such is the way of brass-knuckles capitalism in America.

TWO

How bad can things get? Look around you: Companies laying-off employees by the thousands and shipping their remaining high-paying jobs to China and India and Mexico. Thousands of wage earners losing their homes, victims of foreclosure. Millions more who owe more on their mortgages than their properties are worth, and stretching their meager pay to put food on the table for their families. Fat cat hedge fund firms, where the big money is, more interested in squeezing a buck out of options and derivatives and interest rate swaps than investing in new plants and businesses. Escalating grocery and gas and clothing prices. Healthcare costs beyond what most Americans can afford and climbing annually. Thirty-five thousand lobbyists pressuring 535[1] members of Congress and all those Administration hotshots for special favors and getting them in exchange for campaign donations and luxury Caribbean cruises. The average CEO receiving more than 500 times what the typical worker makes. Get the picture?

The Huffington Post printed a story about an investment banker who threw a hissy fit when he

---

[1] 435 members of the House of Representatives plus 100 senators

found out he was getting a bonus of one million dollars. Seems the poor fellah was expecting double that. Know what the spoiled brat did? He stormed into the executive john, shit on the floor, ran his shoes through it and walked through the executive suite's plush carpeting. So, don't tell me money isn't an obsession. There is an elite class infatuated with it and hell bent to get it.

Then there's the rest of us. Corporation white-collar workers like me, small franchise owners and car salesmen, all fixated on $50,000 cars, 3000 square foot homes in ritzy neighborhoods and exorbitantly over-priced high fashion clothes with names like Gucci and Prada. As if we could afford it. Foolish white-collar workers one step ahead of bankruptcy court and still unable to stop our out-of-control spending. Urged to spend, spend, spend with money we don't own and never will.

~ ~ ~

When I finally stumbled into my upscale three-thousand-square-foot home in a glitzy Duluth neighborhood at 8:00 p.m., my wife Laura Lee confronted me before I had a chance to sneak past her and crawl up the stairs and go to bed. She planted herself directly in my path, blocking the way, and said in a voice as chilly as an Alaskan night, "You're late. We'll barely have time to make the Jefferson's dinner party."

"I'm not in the mood to go."

"Damn it, Sam, we made a commitment. They're expecting us." She stopped abruptly and strode closer to me, frowning, her eyes focused on my face. "Where the hell have you been, anyway?" She sniffed the air. "Jesus, you've been drinking."

"Better believe it." Fortified by booze, I was in no mood for anybody's bullshit.

Laura Lee was all too familiar with my struggle with the bottle, an on-again, off-again problem since the death of my daughter. I staggered into the living room and collapsed onto the closest chair. After two years of utter sobriety, I had stepped off the wagon tonight. With a vengeance. My head was swimming from the boilermakers, shots of scotch chased by tap beer. At that moment, I didn't give a royal damn about the Jefferson's dinner party, what Laura Lee thought about me or the state of this fucked-up world.

"Leave me the hell alone," I snarled.

She stood in front of me like an imperious Roman soldier, impatiently tapping her foot on the parquet flooring, her eyes flashing anger. Her finely spun blonde hair was done up in a beehive hairdo that accentuated the delicate features of her face: chiseled nose, high cheekbones, long unlined brow. The black evening dress she wore with a string of pearls around her neck finished the picture: a cultured woman, one accustomed to the finer things in life: a beautiful home, dinner parties, the theatre, everything her apparent social status in life required.

Except it was all phony, a facade. The woman was a con artist supreme. Told me she came from solid southern stock. I thought I was getting prime rib. Instead I had bitten into a greasy burger.

Laura Lee O'Hara, née Scruggs, came from redneck stock near the peanut farms of South Georgia.

No Jobs Available

From a place where they're still fighting the Civil War at Wednesday night Masonic meetings, and the word "Yankee" never trips from the tongue without a dash of venom. And I was a Yankee from Rhode Island.

She was the product of an outlaw family that barely managed to stay one arm's length away from the sheriff's handcuffs. Genuine trailer park trash. Petty thieves, drifters, flimflam men and women. Inherited traits she used to considerable advantage when it came to hooking me.

Normally, I gave in to her. Anything to avoid an argument. But not tonight. "You want to go to the Jefferson's dinner party, go by yourself, *Pudge*."

She froze. Pudge was the name her corrosive sorority sisters pinned on her during her first year at Evermore Institute, a small hick college in southern Georgia, at a time when Laura Lee was overweight. She hated to be called Pudge, and I knew it and she knew I knew it. Boozing made me say and do awful things. One of the reasons I had gone on the wagon to begin with. A pang of guilt shot through me.

Laura Lee was my second wife and my first mistake at marriage. Three years ago, my first wife, Margaret, despondent from the death of our daughter Cindy packed her bags and moved to San Diego to live with her sister.

Two months later the divorce papers arrived. She left me with the house but took almost all our savings with her. That event, coming three years after the car wreck that killed my lovely daughter Cindy tipped me back over the edge again into the consoling abyss of booze. The only reason I didn't stay immersed in booze was because Freddie took charge of my life and made sure I didn't succumb to the bottle.

But my divorce left me shaken and off-balance, vulnerable and ready for anything. To say I leaped into marriage with Laura Lee would be the understatement of the century. Hungering for companionship and hurting deeply from Margaret's abandonment, I made the unforgivable, half-witted mistake of marrying the first woman who showed an interest in me. At twenty-nine, twenty-two years my junior, Laura Lee bedazzled me. I found her attentiveness and sexual allure more than a desperately lonely middle-aged guy could resist.

I didn't know she was knocked-up at fourteen during a gang bang with four members of the high school football team, which one the father she never found out. Didn't know she abandoned the baby. Didn't know she spent the next fourteen years bouncing from one bum to the next. Didn't know she had two former boyfriends rotting away in state slammers.

And now that it was too late, I *did* know why she never married. I was the first sucker with a good job she found who was stupid enough to fall for the bait.

The woman was self-centered, lazy and uncaring. Never once during our unhappy two years of marriage had she considered the possibility of contributing to the upkeep of our expensive lifestyle. Instead she watched TV, gossiped with the neighbors, and although I was never able to prove it, played hide the social sausage with neighborhood teenage boys.

"Sam, you swore before God when we married you wouldn't drink anymore."

I looked over her shoulder, at the ceiling,

anywhere but into her piercing eyes.

"You gave me your word."

"Why don't you take the hint and leave me be?"

"Are you going to the Jefferson's with me or not?"

"Goddamn it," I roared, fed up now and ready to blow off some steam. "I got fired today."

Laura Lee turned pale and her lips twitched. She said nothing, apparently too stunned to speak. It was the only time I could recall having been able to shut her up.

"The company was bought out. They're closing down purchasing jobs at corporate headquarters."

Laura Lee fell into a chair across from me. The shock registered in her eyes. She knew, as well as I, how little we had in savings. The financial nut on the house alone was enough to crack us in six months.

"How much severance did you get?"

I sighed. "Three months."

She turned even paler. "That can't be right. You've given Bowkart nine years."

"Believe me, it's right. Donna and Charley got even less."

Her voice turned cold. "I don't care about Donna and Charley."

"Of course you don't."

She ignored the reproach in my voice, maybe never even heard it. She was still in a state of shock, too wrapped-up in her own self-absorbed world. Now a world of hurt.

"Any chance of you getting a job in one of the plants?"

"Forget it. Not going to happen."

"What're we going to do?"

"The insurance," I said, "is what worries me most."

"A year?"

"One month."

Her mouth dropped. "That can't be." Laura Lee understood the implications. My diabetes was bad enough. Should any other serious medical complication befall either of us we'd be in deep doo doo. Even the simplest operation today cost thousands of dollars. Ten years ago, a surgeon removed three polyps from my colon, a simple outpatient procedure lasting forty-five minutes, at a cost of $4500. That same simple surgical procedure today costs $20,000. And the cost of drugs is outrageous. The pharmaceutical and insurance companies were gouging the American people, and politicians, obliged to them for cash campaign contributions that would have choked a horse, were allowing them to get away with it.

Answering Laura Lee's probing questions was driving me to the edge of sobriety. I rose unsteadily and said, "I'm going back out for a drink."

"You can't." She bounced to her feet and put her hands on her hips. The gesture stirred memories of my drill instructor in Marine Corps boot camp, so many years ago, hands on his hips, chewing out our dumb recruit asses. "We've got to figure a way out of this," she said.

"There isn't any."

"You're acting defeatist."

"Right now, I'm feeling defeatist."

"If you keep on drinking we'll never figure this out."

I spun around to face her. "You don't get it, do you? There is no easy way out. I'm fifty-one-years-old. Who's going to hire a washed-up relic like me when they can get somebody twenty years younger at half the salary?"

"There's got to be some money somewhere. Don't tell me you don't have some cash squirreled away."

"There's nothing you don't already know about." And there wasn't. Damn the bitch for her suspicions.

"How about your boss, Freddie? He got you into this mess. Hit him up for a loan. You don't have to pay it back, you know."

"You disgust me."

She put a hand on my arm to restrain me. I shook it off and strode back into the night.

~ ~ ~

Laura Lee left me the following week. I came home late one afternoon after dropping off my resume at a half-dozen recruiting agencies in Buckhead and Dunwoody, and Laura Lee was gone. Just like that. I searched the house for a written note or message on the digital recorder and found nothing. Her closets were empty as well as the chests of drawers containing her clothes. She left not only with her own jewelry but also the two nice pieces my mom left me: a gold wristwatch and an emerald broach, both worn by my first wife, and now Laura Lee. To make matters worse, she drove off in the Lexus and left me the battered seven-year-old Chevy pickup truck.

I called the cops and reported the stolen property.

They sent out a squad car and two bored cops wrote down my claim. Not that I thought reporting Laura Lee would do any good. A virtual crime wave was sweeping the country in the wake of the economic downturn. Cops everywhere, particularly those in the larger cities, were swamped with complaints. Far too many to handle. My piss ant problem was minor compared to the daily flood of burglaries, hold-ups and thefts they had to contend with.

About the only thing I could count on was that I had one less burden: The biggest mistake I ever made was finally out of my life.

THREE

"Another martini?" the bartender asked me.

"That, sir, is a philosophical question," I slurred, already shitfaced at four in the afternoon. "You see, my good man, I normally prefer scotch. But today is an exception. So, what might be considered best, the bard asks the bartender, scotch or that amazing concoction known as a martini?"

"You're doing a pretty good job on those martinis," the bartender said with a trace of sardonic amusement. "Why don't you stick to those? Scotch on top of martinis will knock you on your kiester."

"Very well, then," I replied in a fake upper class British accent, "be a good fellow and bring me another one of those marvelous libations."

"Coming up."

I turned my attention to the TV set over the bar. It was tuned to one of those late afternoon cable TV business shows, the sort that profiles business leaders of well-known companies. Today the interviewer, a young suck-ass kid with a cultivated prep school accent and a feigned smile, was salivating over the success of L. Winfred Hurlington, chairman and CEO of Shaley International, the company that was acquiring my former employer. Five minutes into the interview and the kid's nose was already buried so deep up Hurlington's ass it might never again breathe fresh air.

I was watching this disgusting spectacle from a not-so-comfortable barstool, so I shifted my weight around to reposition myself. The pervasive smell of barroom beer made me wrinkle my nose. This wasn't the highest class drinking establishment in the area, but the cost of its drinks was the lowest.

"Mr. Hurlington," the suck-ass kid said, "may I inquire about your philosophy of managing people?"

Hurlington's face was a picture of sustained arrogance, the kind that gets that way after years of being told by ass-kissing subordinates how wonderful his majesty is and how perfect his judgment.

"I believe in objectively evaluating employees in a clear light devoid of favoritism, and I expect every manager in this company to do the same for their subordinates. That includes, of course, the managers of our most recent acquisition, Bowkart Industries, USA." Hurlington stopped for a moment, and steepled his fingertips. "To achieve that end, I consider employees, from top executives on down, as either performing or non-performing assets of the corporation. The performing assets we nurture, the others, well ..." He frowned and his voice trailed off.

The suck-ass kid's head was bobbing up and down in rapid-fire agreement. "Yes, I think I understand. That sounds like a fair and balanced way to evaluate how well employees perform to expectations. Can you give me an example?"

Hurlington thought for a moment and looked down his nose at the suck-ass kid. "Assume you have a well-performing common stock in your personal portfolio, and that stock is in a growth industry. If the company has a top-notch management team, your obvious course of action is to increase your holdings and add to your portfolio. However, if one of your stocks turns out to be a company with a disappointing record of earnings that shows no signs of improving, and the company's management record is unimpressive, the obvious choice is to dump the stock for whatever price the market will bear. To cut your losses, if you will."

The suck-ass kid squinted in an attempt to appear thoughtful. His face brightened, as if the words streaming from Hurlington's thin lips were nuggets of platinum-plated wisdom. "What an astonishing insight."

"That's exactly how we handle our employees. I can't think of an eminently fairer way to rate them. Perform or leave. Evaluating employee performance through that objective prism eliminates subjective bias such as displayed by supervisors who allow personal likes and dislikes to influence the ratings of their subordinates. That about sums it up, young man."

That summed it up all right. Were I the interviewer I would have asked this question: "If that's true, Mr. Hurlington, why did the board of directors award your sorry ass a seventy-million-dollar bonus last year when your company suffered a loss for the same period? Who was the non-performing asset then?" But, of course, I wasn't the interviewer. And the suck-ass kid wasn't about to ask that question. Not in a million light years.

"What a bunch of happy horseshit. These top-level

corporate types sound exactly like weaseling politicians." This came from the guy sitting to my right at the bar in response to the interview on TV. I listened in while sipping my martini and staring straight ahead at the mirror behind the bar.

"Don't you ever know it," came the rejoinder from another guy nursing a double whiskey on the other side of him. "Reminds me of what a political writer once said about Republicans."

"What's that?"

"Well, to para ... para ... something –"

"To paraphrase."

"Yeah. Anyway, this guy, I think his name's O'Rourke, said Republicans are always bitching that government doesn't work, then they get in office and prove it. Same goes for Democrats, you want my opinion. Economy's so fucked up now, I don't think it's ever going to recover."

The other guy snickered and glanced around suspiciously. "Hey, be careful what you say. The walls have ears."

"Yeah, you're right," the other guy whispered back in a hoarse whiskey-soaked voice.

A telling point. In this day and age of the Patriot Act and relentless surveillance, one needed to be ever so careful about expressing any controversial opinion in public or in private, particularly a point-of-view that reflected poorly on the current inhabitants of the federal government. Disgruntled citizens who shot their mouths off were losing their jobs and being arrested and tossed in the can in the belief that everybody is guilty until proven innocent. Civil liberties be damned. Freedom of speech, once a constitutional given, was rapidly deteriorating under the ferocious governance of a suspicious government. In that respect, the current Democratic administration was no better than the previous Republican administration.

"If you appreciate my political insights so much," the first drinker said, "I have another one for you."

"Uh oh."

"In American business and politics, shit rises to the top."

The other drinker tugged at the first drinker's sleeve and looked in my direction to see if I was listening. "Goddamn it, watch your mouth," he said, "You'll get us both in trouble."

My cell phone rang. I turned away from the TV and the telltale conversation next to me and answered it.

"Mr. O'Hara?" a woman asked, sounding both pleasant and impersonal at the same time. The quintessential corporate voice.

"Yes, speaking."

"I'm Sally James, director of human resources for Gilmore Electronics. You've heard of us?"

My interest quickened. "Sure, who hasn't? Your company's one of Atlanta's largest high-tech employers."

"The largest, as a matter of fact. You sent us a resume about a purchasing position. Can you possibly come in to see me tomorrow afternoon at 2:00 p.m.?"

"Let me check my calendar." My heart began to hammer like a piston gone wild. I took a deep breath, held it for a moment and slowly let my breath out to calm myself. I held up my empty pocket organizer to the cell phone and riffled some pages loud enough for the woman to hear. "Looks like I'm free tomorrow afternoon."

"Good. Then it's settled. When you check in at the receptionist, please ask for me."

"I'll do that. And thank you."

We hung up. My heart was still thudding. I reached for the martini and took a giant sip with shaking hands. This was my first break in two months of job hunting. To say I was reaching a state of desperation would not be an overstatement. I was rapidly approaching the only time in my entire working life without a paycheck. What little money I had in my bank account was rapidly thinning, and I had one month left of severance pay. My home, an expensive burden, was listed with a real estate agent, but in a depressed market, it stood little chance of being sold. In the meantime, the cost of diabetic supplies – not covered by the government's health insurance plan – was steadily chipping away at what little money remained in my bank account.

Finding another job. Jesus. My first two weeks out of work, I touched base with every name in my Blackberry, contacts I developed over nine years of working for Bowkart Industries, USA. And I had contacts up the gazoo.

I was clever about it, never once embarrassing the executives I telephoned by asking them for a job. Rather, I explained my circumstances, related my accomplishments and asked if they knew of any company hiring purchasing professionals. Obviously, I was fishing for openings in their companies, but would never come right out and say so. Didn't want to back anyone into a corner. Executives are sensitive to such pressure and they have long memories. Besides, it would have been humiliating for me to go begging.

All to no avail. No matter how many businesspeople I talked to or how hard I tried, I couldn't generate any interest or referrals. The market was that dry.

Once my days of employment came to an end, it shocked me to find out how many of my so-called business friends wouldn't take my phone calls. Those who did, brushed me off. Fair weather friends all. Not that I should have expected any different. Most business friends are exactly that: friends as long as the business connection remains open. Close that connection and the so-called friendship shuts down with it.

The few who actually took my calls were pressed for time and anxious to end the telephone conversations. Another dead-end and another kick-in-the-ass welcome to the world of reality.

Next, I tried the resume route. Results: nada, niente, nothing. Despite having sent out literally hundreds by e-mail or by snail mail either directly to companies or to recruiters, I was striking out. My lack of success in getting a single interview, less a job offer, shook me to the core. The economy was so piss-poor that white-collar jobs of any stripe were at a premium. Add to that dismal scenario the fact that I was in my fifties and out-of-work, and the picture was bleak. My prospects were as dim as the growing legion of homeless people clogging the streets of every major American city and suburb.

Had I been an upper level manager like Freddie I might have attracted more attention. Executives at the vice president or director level, especially those under fifty with a record of accomplishment, seem to land faster than salaried employees at a lower level of the organization, such as supervisors or middle managers. Let's face it, I told myself, you're a purchasing specialist with little managerial experience, and you've been set adrift in an economy where few corporate purchasing jobs exist.

I must admit there was an even more insidious factor at work. For people my age it's often difficult to learn new tricks. I guess it has something to do with how viewpoints calcify over time. You arrive at middle age with a fixed set of ideas and beliefs, and it takes a ton of explosives to blast through the barrier of your experiences. In other words, it becomes extraordinarily difficult to change. Your viewpoints harden into concrete.

No matter how much you try to hide it, your unwavering position on any number of issues somehow manages to surface during interviews. Clever human resources managers understand this phenomenon and probe for it carefully, particularly with older job candidates, to see how much they're set in their ways, and how much flexibility they've lost along the way.

The interview tomorrow was my first shot at a job. With luck and a little help from the man above, I might pull it off. I pushed the empty martini glass aside and went home to sober up.

FOUR

"Mr. O'Hara?"

"Yes?" I stood and faced the woman who asked the question. She was ash blonde, in her late thirties and dressed in a gray business suit.

"I'm Sally James. Would you come with me, please?" No smile, appraising eyes, all business.

I followed her through the lobby and into the carpeted offices of Gilmore Electronics, one of the many high tech companies that sprouted during the nineties in Atlanta, and one of the few to make a go of it in the current economic downturn.

I was dressed in a conservative dark blue suit with pastel blue shirt and striped tie, black loafers, and I carried a slim Hartmann attaché case: standard corporation garb for interviews.

Once in her office, Ms. James slid into a chair behind her walnut desk and signaled me to take a seat in front. I sat down and nervously wiped the cold sweat from my hands against the seams of my trousers, hoping she wouldn't notice. Behind her, on the wall, two framed certificates attested to her undergraduate degree from Ohio State and her MBA from Georgia State University.

We sat in silence for a couple of minutes while she reviewed my resume. Finally, she placed it on her desk, leaned back and examined me with cold gray eyes. Not a flicker of a smile crossed her lips. I was looking at a zombie for all the life she showed.

"Mr. Adamson asked me to interview you," she said, and I detected a whiff of resentment. Charles Adamson was senior vice president of operations and the executive to whom I mailed my resume. Evidently, Ms. James objected to unsolicited resumes coming in to Gilmore Electronic executives other than her.

"I would have sent the resume directly to you, Ms. James, but I wasn't aware–"

"No need to apologize, Mr. O'Hara. Shall we get on with the interview?"

"Of course."

"Why were you fired from Bowkart Industries, USA?"

Got right into it, didn't she?

"I wasn't fired. I was laid-off. Along with three-thousand other employees."

"But many other employees were retained."

"Sure, but –"

"Including other purchasing people."

I stumbled my way through an explanation of how the plant purchasing people weren't let go, just the corporate overhead. She wasn't listening.

"You have no college degree."

"I have a two-year community college degree in business earned while I was in the Marine Corps."

The corner of her lips turned down. "A correspondence course."

"From a fully accredited college."

"But no four-year degree."

"That's true. Still, I have over twenty years of productive manufacturing experience, the last nine of those years in purchasing."

"But none in the electronics industry."

"Ms. James, I'm an experienced and very competent purchasing professional and –"

"Your experience has been in corporate staff. Our opening is in a plant location, and the new purchasing agent will be held directly responsible for results. We don't have any corporate purchasing function as such. We do employ a small corporate group, and that group is composed of mainly financial professionals."

"As I said, my whole career was in manufacturing, most of it at the plant level."

"But none in purchasing at the plant level, which is what we're talking here, isn't that correct?"

I was beginning to sweat and prayed she wouldn't detect it. "Well, when I worked as an industrial engineer in the manufacturing department I often evaluated what machinery to buy in conjunction with the plant's purchasing agents."

"You covered the technical side, reviewing specifications, that sort of thing. Is that right?"

"Yes, that's correct."

"But you didn't negotiate with machinery vendors on pricing. The purchasing people did that."

And so it went. Ms. James would raise a question regarding my capabilities or experience, and I'd answer it while trying not to appear defensive, although her questions sounded more like attacks than the usual probing questions designed to uncover experience and capabilities.

Ten minutes later the interview was over. Ms. James escorted me to the lobby with a flip, "We'll be getting in touch with you."

Yeah, sure.

~ ~ ~

What a crushing disappointment. I had foolishly allowed my expectations to build. I should have known better.

What most job applicants don't realize is that human resource (HR) managers are in the business of screening prospective job candidates *out*, not *in*. Here's how it goes: a company advertises in the local newspaper for, say a cost accounting supervisor, and receives 1000 responses, not an unusual number of replies during a tight job market. The HR manager sorts resumes the company receives in response to the ad. Each is placed into one of two piles: discard or further review. About 900 of those resumes will find their way into the discard pile for any number of reasons: wrong industry experience, no cost accounting experience, too many jobs, sloppy resume, not enough focus on accomplishments and so forth.

The next step involves a more careful screening, one in which the HR manager reads the 100 remaining resumes line by line and places each into one of the same two piles: discard or further review. Now the screening criteria tighten up considerably: Does the candidate have the right kind of cost accounting experience? Does he or she have industry experience? And so on. Maybe twenty-five job candidates make the cut.

Next comes the first interview, assuming the job candidate's resume has succeeded in passing through the initial filters. Nowadays much of that interviewing is done online. As silly as it sounds, and it is silly – how much can you learn about a job candidate by the way he answers online questions – it's just another way for HR to screen out candidates. The objective is to winnow the candidate pool to about a dozen prospects.

In the subsequent step the HR manager conducts phone interviews with the purpose of further winnowing the candidate pool to about four or five candidates. It's almost as silly as online interviews. After all, how much can you learn in a ten-minute telephone conversation other than the timbre of the candidate's voice? I've known some HR types who rejected job candidates during phone interviews because (1) they didn't have executive-sounding voices, (2) they stuttered. What job candidate wouldn't be nervous, speaking to a disembodied voice? (3) they paused too long when the HR type asked questions. I guess it's a sin to think before speaking, and (4) they asked the HR type too many times to repeat their questions. Often the connection is bad, especially when using cell phones. If you're unlucky enough to catch a bad connection, you're road kill.

Then, and only then, are the remaining job three or four candidates offered the opportunity to visit the company for interviews.

This winnowing-out process has led many job hunters to cynically modify the name "Human Resources Manager" to "Inhuman Resources Manager." I'm not one of those. In my opinion the way HR people operate is inherent to the nature of the hiring process and the vast number of job candidates who apply for work. But I do have a quarrel with the absurdity of online screening centered on answers to boilerplate questions that reveal nothing relevant to the job, and the use of telephone interviews to reject what might be viable, even outstanding, job candidates on the basis of their voices.

In my case, I was winnowed-out. In spades. Ms. James kept on chiseling away until she found more than enough black marks to disqualify me from even a janitorial job in her company. Of course, the woman was royally pissed-off that I went over her head and sent a resume to one of the vice presidents of the company. But, had I sent my resume to her, she most likely would have filed it in the trash basket. Sorry, no job openings. A catch-22. In any case, the minute Ms. James showed me the door, I knew that my first and only interview since being laid-off was a sham and a bust.

Back to square one. I drove away in my battered pickup truck to the nearest gin mill.

FIVE

The bank officer twitched his nose. I prayed that he couldn't smell the alcohol on my breath. Despite the package of breath mints I chewed up, I wasn't sure the damned things fully covered the fetid reek of booze.

"I see you're asking for an equity loan in the neighborhood of ... let' see, oh yes, $12,000. To cover your house payments for the next four months."

"Actually, to tide me over until I sell the house."

"You've had your house on the market now for ..."

"Three months." I was beginning to sweat.

He looked up from the loan application and his gaze swept over me. I was wearing my interview suit so I knew my buttoned-down appearance would meet with his approval. What I was less certain about was the impression my bloodshot eyes left, or the sense of desperation that exuded from me as palpable as a kick in the shin. The aloof attitude of the bank officer didn't help.

"I'm not trying to discourage you, Mr. O'Hara, but right now the market is so depressed, it may take a couple of years to sell your house. If then."

I cleared my throat. "The real estate agent feels he can find a buyer within the next few months."

"I see." But I could tell from the way he shifted his gaze away from me, he didn't. The man wasn't stupid. He knew I was lying. My spirits began to slide downhill faster than a bobsled plummeting through a luge. I gripped the arms of my chair to keep my hands from shaking.

"According to what I see, your house is fully leveraged. And your asking price is way too high to attract a serious buyer."

"I intend to lower the price soon."

"You already have a mortgage on the house with Prime Bank of Atlanta, which means they'd have first call in the case of an ... insolvency."

How nice of him to remind me.

"Frankly, Mr. O'Hara," the bank officer continued, "there's no way we can collateralize the loan using your house. As for your other assets" – he emphasized the word assets as though it were a joke – "there's simply not enough there to cover the loan requirements."

"Look, even if I can't sell the house fast, I'm close to landing a job. That means a steady income and –"

"In today's economy, gambling on getting a new job to cover a loan is a risky business. One this bank is not prepared to take. Besides, we have our own problems. You'd be surprised at the number of loans we have in default."

"Yeah." As if I gave a rat's ass about everybody else's problems. I had enough of my own to contend with.

Both of us stopped talking and stared at each other across the expanse of his desk, like boxers resting between rounds, eyeing their opponents across the ring. His expression remained neutral. Mine, I knew, showed every inch of my fury. He blinked and turned away.

There was nothing more to be said. I clenched my jaw shut, knowing I was close to spewing out my true feelings. Instead, I rose hastily and left the bank.

~ ~ ~

In Atlanta, leaves fall from the trees a month or two later in the season than in the colder northern climates of the country. Around me, oak trees were still partially clad with leaves, in the final stages of undressing and exposing their naked limbs to the world for all to see before they closed down for their winter siesta. Poplars, silver maples and birches were already fast in slumberland.

My assets, as the bank officer so kindly brought to my attention, were below subsistence levels and rapidly approaching zero. Thankfully, I had kept the house in my name when I married Laura Lee. About the only semi-smart thing I did while living with the lady. Other than that, there was a dispiriting $1904 in my checking account and an old pickup truck with a Blue Book value of maybe $500. Some furniture in the house I might sell at garage-sale prices. The money in my savings accounts had evaporated, consumed by day to day living expenses. I was living – existing is a better word – on unemployment payments that covered food, gas for my car, toilet paper and not much else.

The only significant asset I owned was the house. Though the equity I had in it, about $50,000, was a mirage. Even if I could sell it, the price was certain to be low enough to lose most or all of my investment.

I was already reduced to the subsistence level for

my two daily doses of insulin. Every morning at 6:00 a.m. and every afternoon at 5:00 p.m. I reported to the county health department to receive free shots. This twice-a-day ritual consumed about two hours of my time since the county health department was already swarming with low income and homeless people getting free medical help, and I had to wait my turn. Time I could ill afford since it detracted from job hunting during prime working hours.

I even considered contacting Freddie to request help. Maybe he could provide a contact or two. But I knew deep down that was wishful thinking. Freddie had supplied Charley, Donna and me with a list of contacts before we left Bowkart. I went through them the first few days after being laid-off.

A crisis loomed over me like a cloud of poisonous gas. I was in frantic need of a job, any job, unless I wanted to sleep under a bridge and forage for scraps of food like so many other homeless Americans. Or live in those God-awful tent cities and risk being assaulted and robbed, beaten-up, even killed.

Were my father alive today, he would have kicked my ass. There was a man blinded by the glitter of materialism. From the time I was a pre-teenager, he tried to instill in me the importance of gathering assets, particularly liquid assets such as cash, bonds and stocks.

He was second generation Irish, an only child, reared dirt poor in the slums of Providence, by a drunken mother and father, both who depended on the welfare of others to survive. Never once did my old man take to drink or drugs, probably as a reaction to his parents who stayed perpetually drunk until their late fifties when cirrhosis of the liver killed them both. I never knew my grandparents, and from what my father told me about them, I was probably better off.

About four years before his parents died, my old man quit high school, left home and became an apprentice to a carpenter in South County, Rhode Island, working for him at below minimum wage. The carpenter owned a potato farm and he let my old man live in a room off his barn, rent-free, for the two years he worked there.

Afterward, he struck out on his own as a journeyman carpenter, hiring out to local construction companies. Flush with cash from his first real job, he married an immigrant Italian girl. No sooner had they settled in East Greenwich, Rhode Island, a middle-class town bordering on Narragansett Bay, when his wife gave birth to me, their only child.

My old man was a fine craftsman and soon had a growing number of customers providing him steady work. But the insecurity of his earlier years ate away at him, eroding his ability to relax and enjoy life. Instead, he started his own small home construction company and hired other carpenters to work for him. Obsessed with success, there never was enough money for him. He had to have more. He worked seven days a week, twelve to fourteen hours a day building the business, devoting his entire life to the accumulation of assets.

The need for money and material wealth consumed him. The fancy home in East Greenwich, the Mercedes, the stocks and bonds, the hidden bank account in the Bahamas. We had them all, along with month-long vacations every year to places like Italy and Ireland. Not bad for a shanty Irishman from the wrong side of the tracks, the old man used to say, and he was right.

When I was a senior in high school, we held one of our infrequent father-son-chats. "Money in our society," he told me, "means everything. It's how we measure people. Not by how good they are, although your mother likes to believe that garbage, but by how much they own. Somebody tells you different, they're lying. Or they're stupid. If you never learn nothin' else from me, don't ever forget that."

Implicit in those words was the insinuation I was letting him down by planning to join the Marine Corps after high school instead of going to college or landing a steady commercial job. Meaning I lacked what it took to reach out and grab the prize, the money. Maybe that was true as he saw it, but as much as the old man cherished material things, I didn't have the same hunger. Not that I wanted to live poor. But neither did I want to devote my entire life to an all-consuming focus on wealth. In that respect, I was more like my mother, who appreciated the material success my old man provided, but wasn't overwhelmed by her need for it.

My attitude now was 180 degrees different. Since losing my job I was sure the old man had nailed it, that I shouldn't have been so hard-headed. I didn't realize that nothing in corporate life is permanent. That within a moment's notice, a snap of the fingers, and despite many years of productive work, you could lose your job. Without money or other assets, I didn't have anything to fall back on to tide me over. I was just another complacent white-collar wage slave living a false dream.

Now that I was forced to think about it, I was the type of personality that harbored lingering doubts about my ability. I suffered twinges of jealously when an associate moved ahead in business or a neighbor moved into a bigger house in a better neighborhood. At those times, I couldn't help but wonder if the old man wasn't right, after all. I guess you can never wipe your personal slate clean of the influence of your parents. My father was a strong influence on my life, and he understood the importance of money. I didn't, but, as the saying goes, I came to maturity later than most, and lived to regret not heeding his good advice.

My old man's obsession with wealth ultimately turned to greed, and that's when it caught up with him.

That ugly Saturday in August is burnished in my memory. The IRS raided our home, handcuffed the old man and led him away to jail. The government ultimately convicted him of tax evasion. From that moment on, it was poverty row for Mom and me. The government stripped us to the bone. We lost our home, cars and our good names. Even the hidden bank account in the Bahamas which evidently wasn't so well hidden that the IRS couldn't find it. The loss destroyed my old man. In the second year of a five-year term for income tax evasion, prison doctors found a cancerous lump on my old man's back. In six months he was dead. Doctors told me I couldn't connect the event of his trial and prosecution with the disease, but I think otherwise. I'll always believe that the cancer was the direct result of his fall from grace.

His death was all the bad news Mom could handle. Twenty-six days later, a sudden heart attack killed her. So, at seventeen, I was on my own, cast adrift. Two days after scattering Mom's ashes from Newport Bridge, I joined the Marine Corps.

SIX

"Can I be frank, Mr. O'Hara?"

"Sure, fire away." I sat up straighter in my chair. When a recruiter says he's going to be frank, it's normally a preamble to bad news.

"You're at a good age, fifty-one, and you've got an in-depth background in purchasing. Those are the good points."

"I suppose you want me to ask, 'What are the bad points?'"

The recruiter lowered his head and peered at me over his reading glasses. "I was just getting to that."

"Sorry, didn't mean to interrupt."

"The bad news is you're fifty-one and you've got an in-depth background in purchasing."

We sat across an old wooden desk that looked as if General Sherman used it during the Civil War. The cubicle we were in was so small, by stretching my arms I could have touched its opposing walls. The voices of other recruiters chattering on the phone drifted in from adjacent cubicles. The entire recruiting office had the appearance of a telemarketing boiler room.

"I don't get it. Why is that bad news? I know purchasing inside out, both at the plant and corporate level. That's got to be worth something,"

"Let me lay it out for you." He took off his glasses and twirled them in his fingers as he stared at me.

"Two points. First, at your age you should be a director or vice-president. That's according to how human resource people view you. And they're the ones calling the shots."

"But I'm a specialist."

"Point number two. I'm sure you understand with all the layoffs and downsizing and sending jobs overseas, there's not much call for purchasing agents. I would even go so far as to say that the woods are full of them, most of them unemployed."

"It can't be that bad."

"Believe me, it is. It's my business to know. Which leaves you in a vulnerable position, if you don't mind my saying so."

"So why did you ask me over today? Bad news is all I've heard the past four months." I hated the whine in my voice.

The recruiter leaned back and smiled. "Because I may have something for you."

My spirits soared. "What?" was all I could manage to say.

"Now, don't go getting your hopes up. This isn't that much. But at least it'll get you back on a company payroll."

My spirits dropped about one-third of the distance they had soared.

"It's really only temporary work, but you never know where it will take you."

My spirits plummeted the rest of the way to ground zero. "Temporary work?"

"It's with a temp agency. You'll move around from company to company while working for the them. The great part about it is that with all those companies, you're going to be in position to spot permanent positions before they're advertised on the market."

"What kind of work is involved?"

The recruiter cleared his throat and shifted around in his chair. "Well, a variety ... you know."

"No, I don't know."

"That's really up to the hiring company. Look at it this way, you'll get a lot of exposure to work that may open doors for you."

I'll bet. "How much does it pay?"

"The beginning wage is 10 dollars an hour."

"Jesus, that's all?"

"Like I say, it's a start. Look at the bright side. You'll be working while so many others are collecting unemployment."

"I was making eighty grand a year at Bowkart Industries, USA."

"And with any kind of luck you'll be back making eighty grand a year in no time."

I slumped in my chair. "Yeah, in no time. Sure."

The recruiter's voice sharpened. "Interested or not?"

"How about health insurance?"

"Sorry, that's not on the table as a temporary. But you've got Medicaid, the government health insurance option. Let me repeat, interested or not?"

"What choice do I have? I'll take the interview."

The recruiter clapped his hands. "Good move. You're making the right decision. That will be one-hundred dollars."

"*What?*"

"For my services."

"This is nuts."

"Look, I have a dozen other applicants who'll jump at the chance. Take it or leave it."

I took a deep breath and held my anger in check. "I'll take it."

~ ~ ~

"O'Hara, front and center."

I reluctantly left my hardwood bench in the waiting room of the temp agency and approached Donnelly, the assignment clerk. The deep lines around his mouth twisted his face into a perpetual sneer. Not much fun to look at after an early 5:00 a.m. Egg McMuffin breakfast.

"Report at 6:30 a.m. to the Mackles Hardware Distribution Center. Here's your assignment sheet." He handed me a paper with the company name, telephone number, address and name of a supervisor.

"What kind of work –"

"You'll find out when you get there."

For the past month I had been cooking greasy fries in a fast-food joint, and hated every minute of it. The three-hundred-twenty bucks a week they paid me was slightly better than the three-hundred I could collect on unemployment, not much to get excited about. And neither were near enough to pay my bills. I was quickly draining what little cash left in the bank and becoming more and more despairing.

I knew the temp job was too low-level to open doors to full-time employment, despite what the recruiter told me, the lying prick. Most temp jobs involve slinging heavy crates around a warehouse or shuffling paperwork forms at a clerical desk. I hoped this assignment was the latter. I hadn't done any real physical work since I left the Marine Corps, some 30 years before, and the job in fast food was taking its toll, both on my pocketbook and on my soul.

What most white-collar employees don't understand is the devastating effect menial work has after years of holding a respectable job in a comfortable working environment and taking home a decent paycheck.

When you're on the street looking for white-collar employment and you're short of cash and desperate, no matter how hard you try to push it aside hoping that tomorrow will bring you a new and shining white-collar job, it's difficult to overcome your feelings of insignificance. This is especially true in today's dog eat dog economic environment where middle and upper level white-collar jobs are as scarce as uncirculated silver dollars. You can bust your ass phoning contacts and sending out resumes by the hundreds, but after a while when there is little or no response, you begin to question your self-worth. Every day, confidence in your ability to make a comeback erodes just a little further until finally there isn't any left and you're ready to say to hell with it and resign yourself to living on welfare.

The problem for white-collar workers, especially older white-collar workers, is that time is against them. Every unsuccessful day on the job hunt grinds them down a little bit more. More quickly than they realize, the days add up into weeks, then months, then a couple of years. At that stage they're ready to quit trying and join the dispossessed, those millions of unemployed people who have abandoned all hope of ever finding another job. It was frightening to think I could soon be one of them, with my only remaining prospect living underneath a bridge overpass in the company of other failures, just another homeless person.

Even when out-of-work white-collar workers are fortunate enough to land an interview, and they get in front of the guy or gal interviewing them, their fear shows. It's palpable and it marks them. They know deep down they're not going to be considered for the job. Shit, you can't blame the company interviewer. Such over-the-hill job candidates reek of failure. Who wants to hire somebody who's been beaten down and lost his or her confidence?

So, what do they do? They take a job in a fast food joint where their supervisor is a pimply-faced nineteen-year-old, or ride a garbage truck picking-up trash containers from their neighbors, and hope nobody they know recognizes them. What else is left?

Fall turned to spring and spring turned to summer, and I had yet to find a white-collar job. Talk about desperate. Mackles Hardware Distribution Center, here I come.

~ ~ ~

I hopped in my battered pickup truck and drove to Atlanta's crime-ridden southwest side, passing a succession of pawnshops and other dingy businesses, most enclosed by steel fences topped by concertina wire to prevent burglaries. Vicious Dobermans and pit bulls, struggling to get at passers-by and rip their throats out, clawed at the fences and chewed the steel links until blood ran from their mouths. They gave me the shivers. I drove past them as fast as I could.

Mackles Hardware Distribution Center was a large fenced warehouse with a rent-a-cop guarding the front gate. He gave my assignment sheet a quick once-over, told me where to go and waved me through. I parked the car, entered through the warehouse office, found the supervisor's desk and handed him my assignment sheet.

He grunted and said, "You ever pick and pack?"[2]

"Just burgers and french fries."

"Wise guy, eh?"

"Just let me get to work."

He assigned a wiry gnome-like guy named Hitch to show me the way around. Hitch refused my handshake and smirked, displaying yellow-brown teeth that looked as if they had been extracted from a Budweiser horse.

"Follow me." He led me through the warehouse maze at a breakneck pace, explaining as we went along how to pick the parts orders and pack them. His instructions were short and gruff and incomplete, as if he didn't give a rat's ass if I succeeded at following them, and would in fact be happy to see me fall flat on my face. A far cry from working with caring professionals like Freddy. At the conclusion of the tour he dropped me off at my workstation and scuttled away like a rat chasing a piece of aromatic

---

[2] Removing parts from bins, collating them into one order and packing them for shipment.

cheese.

The pick and pack job could have been done by a robot. In fact, many warehouses and distribution centers in a multitude of industries have automated the process. In such operations, an order is received via computer and the automated pick and pack process takes over. Pre-programmed robots remove ordered parts from numbered bins and drop them in containers that are delivered to shipping stations. Employees at these stations finish by packing the orders for shipment, affix shipping labels and send the ready-to-ship packages down conveyors to trucks where they're loaded and shipped. But not at Mackles. It was all physical labor from start to finish.

Physical labor in a broiling Atlanta summer is nothing to scoff about. July through September brings daily temperatures in the nineties and sometimes over 100. Those temperatures climb several degrees in the enclosed warehouse. A thermometer mounted on a column told me the actual inside temperature was 105 degrees. Apparently, Mackles management didn't think air conditioning for its employees was a necessity.

Three hours later, drenched in sweat and my back killing me, I had just about mastered the pick and pack routine on my own. The warehouse supervisor was all over my ass, cussing me under his breath the couple of times I made a mistake, and tramping away in disgust more than once.

Finally, when I was dead on my feet, the klaxon shrilled through the warehouse signifying lunch hour. I staggered into the men's room, washed my hands, threw water over my face and the back of my neck, looked for the paper towels, didn't find any, dried my hands on the side of my shirt and lurched into the adjacent small plant lunchroom. I looked around and noticed the room hadn't been cleaned in God knows how long. Tables were littered with crumbs from opened lunches and the floor was covered with goo from spilled drinks and who knows what else. The only amenity was a giant overhead cooling fan that kept employees cool but was so loud you wanted to eat fast and leave.

I ate a Babe Ruth candy bar from the vending machine and chased it down with a Diet Coke from another vending machine. Twenty minutes later the klaxon shrilled again and I staggered back to my workstation for the second part of my shift, my back so kinked I could hardly stand erect, and sweat already popping out on my brow.

~ ~ ~

When I returned home that evening my voice mail was flashing the name Sidney Berg. I was so tired I didn't immediately recognize who Sidney Berg was. Then it came to me: the realtor handling my house. I listened to the voice mail. Sidney said he had a buyer for my house and to please call him regardless of how late it was. My mood zoomed from glum to joyful in under five seconds. With trembling hands, I dialed Sidney's number.

"Congratulations, Sam. We have a buyer for your home."

"Sidney, I can't tell you how relieved I am. Finally. Tell me more." I was almost salivating into the phone I was so thrilled.

"The buyer is a cable executive transferred from Minneapolis. Got a nice family. Lovely wife and two teenage kids."

"Sidney, I'm not hearing what I need to know. How about the price?"

There was a dead silence on the line for a few uncomfortable seconds. Sidney cleared his throat. "Little bit of a hitch there. He's only willing to pay $275,000."

"*What?*

"Sam, listen to me. You know how hard it's been to sell your home. It's a buyers' market. You're lucky you even have one offer."

"Might as well give the house away. Shit, I paid $315,000. I'll lose my equity."

"Not all of it, Sam."

"That's not the point. I listed the home for #350,000. Two-seventy-five? Jesus!"

"Sam, let me give you the benefit of my knowledge. You're in a strong buyers' market –"

"I've heard that from you a dozen times."

"Sam, Sam, please listen to me. I've been in this business for almost thirty years. I know the market. This may be your only offer. I suggest you take it."

"Is there any chance of him going higher?"

"I tried to move his bid up but he was adamant. Stone face, in fact. We could lose him. There are lots of homes on the market."

"I may as well give the house away," I grumbled.

"You'll still walk away with about fifteen grand."

Dead silence. I tried to squeeze the phone to death.

"Sam, if that doesn't suit you, you have the option to either keep the house on the market or, if you wish, find another realtor."

Another dead silence. Then, "To hell with it. Accept their offer. I need the money."

SEVEN

None of this resolved my money problem. Sure, I had another fifteen grand from the house closing in my pocket, but that was going to run out sooner rather than later. Compared to the fifty-grand down payment made when I bought the house, my net equity loss was $35,000.

The money I was earning at my temp position was peanuts, not near enough to live on, meaning I would have to dip into the fifteen grand for daily expenses. What to do?

Every Sunday the Atlanta Journal-Constitution ran several pages of want ads, most of them for menial entry level jobs, and every Sunday I went through them ad by ad. The few jobs I responded to got me zero responses in return. A frustrating experience, one that left me sunk in a pit of despair.

But this Sunday an ad caught my eye:

Top level executive career firm seeking candidates to fill $100K and up positions. If you are selected, our CEO, the former president of a large management consulting company, will put you in contact with C-Level executives at prestigious companies nationwide. Furthermore, you will be assigned a vice president to work directly with you to help you customize and guide your job campaign. Please forward your resume including contact information.

What the hell. What have I got to lose? I mailed my resume to the post office box described in the ad.

In the meantime, I returned to my pick and pack warehouse job. My job performance was improving day by day. I could tell because no longer was the warehouse supervisor chewing me out. My back and arms were gradually becoming accustomed to manual labor and no longer ached.

In the meantime, my routine seldom varied. Up every working day at 5:00a.m., a trip to the county health department for my insulin shot, a sumptuous breakfast at McDonalds, report to work at Mackles at 6:30a.m., work until 3:00 p.m. with a twenty-minute lunch break halfway through my shift and two five-minute piss call breaks, one in the first half of my shift, the other in the second half of my shift. Next on the agenda, my second trip of the day to the county health department for an insulin shot, then dinner at a fast-food joint such as Burger King or Kentucky Fried Chicken, and home and in bed by 8:00 p.m., exhausted, frustrated, scared shitless about what the future held for me, tossing and turning and finally a drifting into a restless sleep.

I stopped drinking. Not because I was trying to kick the habit. I simply didn't have enough money. A trip to the local tavern was an extravagance I could no longer afford. Gradually, my hands stopped shaking and I no longer had those agonizing morning hangovers.

I was living in a shabby three-room apartment in a low rent district on the southwest side of Atlanta, not far from my employer, the Mackles warehouse. My neighbors were maids, fry cooks, laborers, clerks and a host of other poor souls, many living on unemployment payments, a step away from eviction. The most frequent visitors to our apartment complex were drug dealers and the cops who pursued them. Quite a comedown from my former lovely home and upscale life in an exclusive subdivision in Duluth.

I didn't see much of my neighbors, didn't care to. Every day, I left before daylight and came back nighttime. I was too embarrassed and bitter and depressed to exchange chit chat with anyone.

Then, out of the blue, about one week after I submitted my resume to the career firm listed in the newspaper, I received a phone call.

"Mr. O'Hara, my name is Elaine Dayton, vice president of human resources for C-Level Careers America. We're one of the top career management firms in the country and the most prominent one in all of the Southeast. You replied to an ad we ran in the Atlanta Journal/Constitution and we're interested in learning more about you. Is this a good time to talk?"

I bolted upright in my kitchen chair. Is this a good time to talk? Oh yes, indeed. "Yes, it is, Ms. Dayton, thank you for calling."

"Your resume attracted considerable attention among our senior executive staff. You have an impressive history of accomplishments with your former employers. You are also at the right age for executive level responsibilities." Ms. Dayton had a cultured voice that brought to mind my second wife, Laura Lee. I could only hope that she, and the firm she represented, were not as phony as Laura Lee.

"The right age?"

"Yes, the right age. Most of the companies seeking talented candidates for their executive suites look for men or women in their early to middle fifties."

"I thought candidates over fifty were considered ... well, over the hill."

Ms. Dayton chuckled. "That's simply not the case. At your age, Mr. O'Hara you have the requisite background and successes that make you a highly eligible prospect."

"That sounds promising."

"Do you mind telling me what your job goal is?"

I hesitated for a moment. "Well, something in purchasing, either at the plant or corporate level."

"May I recommend, Mr. O'Hara that you expand your horizons."

"Expand my horizons? How?"

"You have a wealth of corporate experience that can open doors. It would be to your benefit to consider higher level positions. Our executive team corroborates my endorsement and recommendation. They believe you have what it takes to immediately move up to a C-Level position."

I couldn't believe what I was hearing. C-Level! That meant vice-president or higher. Fantastic news. After the shitstorm of grief over the past several months this was music in my ear. I was overjoyed.

"You mean like vice president of purchasing in a large company?"

"I wouldn't confine yourself to purchasing positions, no matter how high the level. You should open your vistas to general management."

"General management? Do you really think I can land that kind of position?"

"Mr. O'Hara, our firm has helped literally thousands of C-Level executives. I assure you that we can spot the difference between executive caliber candidates and those whose abilities are middle manager or below. We have selected you for our program because your credentials are exceptional. Believe me, you wouldn't have received this call otherwise."

"I'm quite flattered, but what specifically does your company do that's different than an executive recruiter?"

"That's a good question, Mr. O'Hara. Have you ever heard of the hidden job market?"

"No, can't say I have."

"I'll explain that in a moment. But first please let me know what avenues you've been pursuing to find a new position."

I sighed. "The usual, I guess. Answering newspaper and online ads, applying to headhunters, that kind of thing."

"Those are the tired and worn avenues most job candidates select. As you undoubtedly have discovered, those avenues are rarely productive at the executive level. The best high-level corporate positions come as a result of one executive talking with other executives, asking if they know of a high performance professional to fill an opening on his staff. That's what we call the hidden market."

"I assumed that happens sometimes."

"More than sometimes, Mr. O'Hara. At the executive level, we estimate that happens more than 80 percent of the time."

I whistled. "This is an eye-opener. I always thought that most executive positions are filled by headhunters or through answering ads companies run in newspapers."

"You're not alone in that opinion. A wrong one, I might add. Most job candidates are unaware of the successes others have achieved tapping the hidden job market. And that's our specialty, to help candidates of your caliber find executives who can either offer them jobs or help them find executive level job openings among *their* contacts. Look at it this way: through our efforts we may put you in contact with a dozen company presidents. Each of those presidents, in turn, may put you in contact with, say, three other presidents or chief executive officers. That original 12 has now blossomed to 48: the original 12 plus an additional 36. Those 36 presidents in turn, may talk to another two or three other company presidents each. You can see where I'm going. It's essentially a geometric expansion that starts with your single contact at our firm."

"You know, that sounds like a really terrific method for acquiring contacts. I can see the value of the hidden job market now."

"That's exactly what it is, Mr. O'Hara, a terrific method."

"Is there a fee for this service?"

Ms. Dayton chuckled. "That's the real benefit of what we do for you. We begin the process with a consultation that is absolutely free. The purpose of this original consultation is to help position your job search and target select C-Level professionals. Our training methods will then send you on a successful journey to your new executive position."

I chuckled. "Not too long a journey, I hope."

"Many of our executive candidates land a high-paying job within six weeks, and some in as little as a week or two. Overall, our success rate in placing job candidates is one of the highest in the nation. I should add that we are quite proud of our accomplishments."

"What happens after the consultation?"

"That's when you're assigned one of our vice presidents to help you strategize a job campaign designed specifically for you."

"No, I meant is there a fee for any further consultations or the actual training itself?"

"I can assure you, Mr. O'Hara, that the starting package you earn on a job found through our firm will make our nominal fee pale into insignificance. Don't forget, we're talking a C-Level compensation package that includes for the average candidate a base salary, performance bonuses, country club membership, a car, superior health care benefits, a low financing rate for your new home and a host of other perks. We're talking in the $100,000 salary range and up ... usually way up. It's not unusual for our graduates to receive a compensation package worth $250,000."

"That does sound wonderful, but I would still like to know how much the fee is."

"That depends on the program custom-designed to fit your particular circumstance. You'll find out when you meet with our president, Mr. Rex Hanover. He'll explain everything fully."

"Is that the same Rex Hanover who was a linebacker for the Atlanta Falcons?"

"The one and the same."

"I knew he left the team years ago, but I wasn't aware where he went."

"Rex owned and ran a management consulting practice for several years, then started our firm five years ago. He's a gifted businessman. Our company has thrived under his guidance. I think you'll truly enjoy speaking with him. Shall we set an appointment, then? How about this coming Friday at 2:00 p.m.?"

I took a deep breath. "I'll be there. Just tell me where to go."

"I'm glad you see the opportunity, Mr. O'Hara. Not everybody does. That puts you in a select class of far-thinking executives. I know Rex is looking forward to meeting you."

"I'm looking forward to meeting Mr. Hanover, too."

"One more thing. Please, call him Rex. You'll find him easy to get along with."

~ ~ ~

For the first time since I was laid-off from Bowkart Industries, USA I felt some hope. Not much, but enough to sustain me until I met Rex Hanover. Visions of holding a meaningful job again floated through my head like heroin through an addict's veins. My optimism soared, until later that evening when I came down to earth and realized I hadn't yet been offered an executive position, and I better tamper my expectations until I met Rex Hanover and start the training program Ms. Dayton described.

Today was Tuesday. I wasn't meeting Rex until Friday at 2:00 p.m. I prayed the time would go fast.

I was too on edge to sleep well that night.

EIGHT

Rex Hanover greeted me in the lobby of C-level Career USA's suite of offices.

"Sam, my name is Rex Hanover. I'm very happy to meet you. You come well recommended." His commanding baritone voice drew your attention. He beamed at me and gripped my hand and pulled me toward him.

I remembered Rex from his NFL days with the Atlanta Falcons: 6'4", lithe build, about 225 pounds. A lightning fast and hard-hitting linebacker, one of the very best in the NFL. From what I could tell he hadn't changed much since then except for his recognizable blonde hair now graying on the sides, and a few etched lines around his eyes. He was tastefully dressed in a dark blue suit, white dress shirt, striped tie and polished dress shoes. He radiated confidence. The type of executive you often see portrayed in movies about business, but seldom in real life.

"Thanks for inviting me, Mr. Hanover."

"Let's get off on the right foot, Sam. Call me Rex. I really dislike formalities." His face crinkled into a smile.

He led me to his office. What I saw made me whistle to myself. Polished and gleaming Cherrywood furniture, from his desk, and credenza behind it, to a long boardroom table and chairs. A large bay window overlooked the Buckhead section of Atlanta.

Autographed pictures adorned the walls: Rex shaking hands with George W. Bush. Rex and Katie Couric walking side by side on a football field during an interview. The 1991 Atlanta Falcon team posing for its annual picture. Rex shaking hands with the CEO of Coca-Cola. These pictures and about three dozen others of Rex with famous celebrities, athletes, businesspeople and politicians. The whole effect designed, I was sure, to create an impression of both executive grandeur and Rex's connections with the famous and influential.

We sat down on chairs arranged around a coffee table. Rex had his secretary bring us coffee.

"You like football, Sam?"

"It's my favorite spectator sport."

Rex reached down and grabbed a football lying on the floor next to his chair. He tossed it to me. I caught it, glad that I hadn't yet picked up my cup of coffee.

"What you're holding, Sam, is the game ball awarded me in the 1991 wild card game."

"Wow." I couldn't help but be impressed. "I remember that game. Against New Orleans, as I recall."

Rex nodded. "We beat them, 27-20. I had one hell of a game. Six sacks." He chuckled. "Unfortunately, we lost the division championship game the following week to the Redskins."

We both sipped our coffee as I glanced around the office and as Rex reflected on past glories.

"What I like about your background, Sam, is your abundant expertise in purchasing, which is the lifeblood of a manufacturing company. Correct me if

I'm wrong, but if the costs of purchased parts and materials are too high, or if supplier quality is not up to standard, the manufacturing company suffers. Agree?"

"I couldn't agree more."

"A background in a job such as what you held at Bowkart is evidence of an executive who knows how to get things done. A doer. A get-the-job-done type of guy. You obviously understand the importance of details. I can't tell you, Sam, how many candidates I interview who skip over the nitty-gritty and make faulty decisions as a result." Rex shook his head in regret. "They're the ones who don't get the job done and fail or get left behind. I feel sorry for them."

I nodded, taken in by the commanding presence of this guy. "I've seen my share of them, too."

"Your age is also a plus. Most senior executives arrive at the executive suite in their early fifties. Which puts you right smack in that sweet spot."

"Ms. Dayton told me the same thing."

"And that's where our firm can help, Sam. With all the corporate layoffs, American jobs shipped overseas to China and India and Mexico, an ever-increasing number of mergers ... sadly, all of those factors are removing high caliber men like yourself away from the firing line."

"It really hit Bowkart hard. Not only me. My friends and associates with many years of service are out of work and don't know where they can find the next job."

Rex nodded in agreement. "Terrible situation. Now, let's get back to you. What my firm, C-Level

Careers America can do is prepare you for the rigors of executive level job hunting. It's different, much different, than trying to find a middle management position. It takes a certain expertise, a flair if you will, for finding the right company and the *exact* right situation for you. And that's precisely what we will do for you."

"Sure, I get it," I replied inanely. The intense way Rex examined me was intimidating. I felt like a hapless chipmunk about to be devoured by a hawk. *Forget Rex's persona. I've got to look past that and focus on what he can do for me.*

"My staff and I reviewed your background and accomplishments, and feel confident that we can put you in contact with the right type of high level corporate executives who may be in need of somebody with your specific background."

My hopes soared. This was the type of service I should have gone to earlier. Still ... other, less optimistic, thoughts intruded. "What I don't understand, Rex, is how a purchasing specialist like me can be considered for general management positions."

Rex reached over and patted my knee. "Where do you think all general managers and top executives start, Sam?"

I sat there looking dumbfounded, until it dawned on me. "Oh, sure. They all began their careers as specialists."

"Exactly. As manufacturing supervisors, accountants, engineers, purchasing agents, customer service representatives, what have you. And they all worked their way to the top."

"I'm beginning to get the picture, now." But doubts lingered. For one quick moment I had the impression that I was being sold a bill of goods by a master salesman. Then I brushed those unpleasant thoughts aside, caught up in the possibility of landing a top corporate job, and believing in Rex's commitment to making it happen.

Rex stared at me as if he could delve deep inside and discover my latent talents. "Besides large companies, I've also got in mind for you vice president of manufacturing or support services for a smaller firm, one where you could stake an equity position."

"Is that possible?"

Rex looked at me with questioning eyes and snorted. "Is it possible? "Not only is it possible, it's highly likely. Either way, large corporation or small manufacturing company, you're a shoo-in."

His enthusiasm was infectious. I was feeling better by the minute.

"However ... there's always a however, isn't there, Sam?"

The brightness faded. I didn't know what to expect.

Rex held his hand up as if to stop any negative thoughts I might entertain. "We first have to correct some basic problems you have."

I blanched. "Basic problems? What basic problems?"

"Let's start with your resume, Sam. Frankly, it's below par. If I were a hiring executive and I picked up your resume, my first inclination would be to throw it in the trash."

"But ..."

"There's also the matter of how you interview. You come across as lacking self-confidence."

I started to object when Rex held his hand up again. "We can correct that, just as we can correct your interviewing style and your resume. In fact, the object of our training program is to dramatically improve every aspect of your ability to take command of an executive interview and land a top position. Those are skills very few job candidates have."

I felt as if I had been kicked in the teeth. Once my bruised ego subsided and I lifted my chin up from the floor, I realized that Rex's evaluation was probably correct. I had to admit that it had been so many years since I searched for a job, I wasn't aware of how I came across in interviews. I had stumbled through my recent interviews with recruiters. And the lack of assurance Rex described is the kiss of death for landing a new job.

"Okay, Rex, I'm in your hands. What's next?"

Rex leaned forward and looked me in the eyes and threw me a blazing smile. "I've got the greatest faith in you, Sam. Coupled with our training methodology and the C-Level executives we're going to put you in touch with, you're going to score, and score big." Rex paused and reached for my hand and gripped it in a handshake. "Moment of truth, Sam. Are you ready to work with my team and me?"

"I'm eager to get started, Rex. How much is this going to cost me?"

"Good news, Sam. You come on board now, and I

can just about guarantee you a job in 90 days."

"Ninety days? Really?" I fervently wanted to believe him, willed myself to believe it, although deep down I knew that Christmas comes only once a year.

"Yes, 90 days. A C-Level job. And in most cases the starting bonus of your new position will more than cover our fees."

"I didn't realize there would be a starting bonus involved."

"Neither do most of our candidates. They're always pleasantly surprised.' Rex stood and faced me. "Ready to get going?"

I stood up in response. "I certainly am, but you never mentioned the fee."

Rex scoffed. "A measly 12,000 dollars."

My knees buckled and I sat back down. "Twelve grand. My God, that's a lot of money."

"Believe me, Sam, between starting bonuses, a high annual salary and executive bonuses and perks, you'll be far ahead of the game."

"I got to level with you, Rex, that's about all the money I have to my name. I don't know if I can afford it."

Rex sat down and took a deep breath. He appeared deep in thought. "Okay, here's what I'm going to do for you. My associates and I like you, Sam. We like you a lot. How's this? Eight grand up front, and the other four when you start your new high-paying executive job."

I closed my eyes and tried to figure if what little cash I had would last me until I started my new executive position. But what choice did I have?

Nothing other than Rex's offer loomed on the horizon. Anguish and despair were my middle name.

I stood up and shook Rex's hand. "Okay, let's go for it."

NINE

I don't know many white-collar workers who can bear the punishing demands of physical labor. Especially those who have been sitting on their asses in offices for a countless number of years. Their muscles eventually atrophy, turn to flab and they fight for breath climbing a flight of stairs. Elevators become the required mode of transportation in high-rise buildings. Taking the stairs risks a heart attack.

Although no longer working in a high-rise, I was no exception. I was easily thirty pounds over my ideal weight. Unless I buttoned my suit coat, my flabby belly was noticeable. Except now that I was running up and down warehouse aisles in jeans and a khaki work shirt, performing the lowest form of manual labor, my shaking gut was fully exposed for all to see. Other employees tittered behind my back and I cussed them out silently. It was tough enough carrying around a sagging gut. It was worse comparing my out-of-shape body with other employees with trim waists who hustled around the warehouse as fast as Olympic relay runners and never seemed to stop.

But as the days rolled on I ate less fast food and more fruits and vegetables. I discovered that healthy eating was more expensive than junk-food eating. On the plus side, I found myself tightening my belt as the weight peeled off. No longer did I huff and puff thirty minutes into the job and for the remainder of my shift. Now I breezed through my job, handling the workload without losing my breath or without my legs giving out or my back aching. As a side benefit, I handled the heat in the warehouse better. I sweat sure, but not with its accompanying exhaustion.

While things were getting better on the health front, they were getting worse – much worse – on the financial front. My small cash hoard was diminishing rapidly and I feared that my predicament was quickly evolving into a decision of whether to pay my rent or give up my truck and walk to work. There were no local bus routes. Another 40 minutes each way and additional shoe leather I could not afford.

I shook off the negative feelings and focused on the future. The C-Level Careers America training program was scheduled to begin in two weeks. Two weekend days of introductory job hunting skills taught by skilled professional career instructors. Then on to individual coaching sessions after work. I wanted badly to compress time so the training and coaching would go fast and the job interviews start. Rex promised that I would have a job within 90 days. I mentally calculated how long my money would last, and was alarmed to discover it would not extend through the next three months.

Time and money were running out fast. Failure was nipping at my heels.

~ ~ ~

Another dreary work day. Everything was routine until about 2 p.m. I was picking an order from warehouse shelves when a claxon horn ripped through the building. Every worker within sight dropped whatever he was doing and ran for an exit.

"What's going on?" I yelled at the worker closest to me.

"Fire alarm," he shouted back. Just about that time I smelled smoke and saw billows of dark clouds creep across the upper stacks of the warehouse and descend in plumes to the floor. The smell was acrid and stung my nostrils. I held a handkerchief over my nose and followed the man in front of me, racing for the exit from the warehouse to the offices. I was the last man out of the warehouse. The offices were deserted, its employees having apparently fled the building.

As I passed the glassed-in payroll office, from the corner of my eye I observed three packets of banded bills lying on a desk. I wasn't surprised. Mackles paid weekly wages in cash, their procedures out of date as usual and far behind the automated check systems just about every other company used. And today was payday, so I could expect to see cash in the payroll office.

Cash simplified things for employees, but it also invited theft. Payday attracted robbers smart enough to figure out what days Mackles paid its employees and then ambush them after they left work. Every now and then one of Mackles workers would find himself at the point of a gun shortly after leaving the warehouse and venturing onto the dangerous streets on the south side of Atlanta.

As far as Mackles management was concerned, out of sight, out of mind. They wouldn't be held responsible for what happened away from warehouse property.

Nevertheless, employees liked receiving cash instead of a check. Flush with payday cash, workers could stop off for a shot of rye and a beer chaser at a local gin mill and bring the rest of the pay home to mama who shopped and paid the household bills.

When it came to security, Mackles management was far behind the times. The company didn't have security cameras mounted in the payroll office. They were mounted at strategic locations in the warehouse because of insurance requirements. The eye-in-the-sky caught workers faking accidents and claiming insurance benefits. A not unusual circumstance for Mackles employees, none of whom made that much money and who lived week to week pinching pennies and barely scraping by. I sure as hell couldn't fault them for attempting to stick it to an insurance company.

From what I had been told by my fellow warehouse employees, the company once used security cameras in all of the offices, including payroll, but did away with them in a cost reduction drive.

I stopped and looked around me. There was nobody else in the office corridor, and the payroll office was deserted. I stepped closer to the glass window and peered at the bills. It looked like three packets of fifties. My heart accelerated and I froze and I heard Dad's voice: take the money, you chickenshit. No, I answered, I couldn't, I wouldn't. Could I?

"*Screw it.*" I slammed open the office door, scooped up the three small packets, jammed them inside my pants pockets and ran out of the payroll office, my heart thudding uncontrollably. By the time I reached the plant exit I was sweating and shaking and cursing myself for taking such a foolish risk. I jerked open the fire door and left the plant and almost collapsed on the blacktop of the parking lot, coughing and panting. Dazed employees surrounded me and stood back from the building staring in disbelief at the flames and smoke rising from the warehouse. Others, like myself, bent over with coughing fits.

I looked around. Nobody approached me. No security guards raced to cuff me. Nobody eyed me suspiciously. I was home free. I patted my pockets where I had stuffed the bills. *Better get the hell out of here*. I rose sluggishly from the blacktop. After I stopped coughing and caught my breath, I jumped in my old pickup truck and drove home.

Once safely inside my apartment I locked the door and hurried around lowering the window shades, then turned on the lights and unloaded the packets on the kitchen table. The apartment was hot and stuffy. I turned on the tiny window air conditioner that rattled more than it cranked out cool air. How I missed the comforts of central air conditioning.

I tore off the bands and counted the bills. Each stack contained 50 bills, all in fifty-dollar denominations. One-hundred fifty bills in all. The final tally amounted to $7500. All of them previously circulated fifties. No new bills.

I opened a can of diet cola from the fridge and sat at the kitchen table. My hands started shaking so much I needed both of them to bring the can to my mouth. I managed to return the can to the table and sat there staring at the bills until my hands stopped shaking and my racing heart rate subsided. Every now and then I darted a look at the front door, terrified that at any moment I would hear a thunderous knock on the door accompanied by a booming voice shouting, "Police. Open up!"

Doubts crowded my mind. Would anybody suspect I stole the money? Had anybody seen me? In both cases I didn't think so. The office corridor was empty when I pocketed the money from the payroll office. Nobody else was there, and since Mackles didn't have security cameras, there weren't any witnesses.

I had never stolen anything before, even so much as pencils and some paper clips from the Bowkart office. Thanks to the way Mom reared me not once did I cheat on my income tax or chisel money or steal from people.

She was the one who required that I go to church regularly, even though I preferred to play ball or go swimming or just goof off. She was the one who checked my school grades, and when they were below par grounded me until they came up again. She was the one who taught me to respect my elders. The discipline she instilled in me helped me survive my father's death.

What happened? How and when did I lose my perspective? Why have I resorted to thievery? Dear Lord, I'm following in my old man's footsteps. The sins of the parents visited on their children. Made me want to cry. My guts were churning. I didn't know which way to turn.

Regardless of my torment, I knew I'd couldn't and wouldn't return the money. Mackles management wouldn't forgive me and the cops would surely arrest me. There was no way out other than to hide the money. But where?

I couldn't put it in the bank. Any sudden infusion of cash into a bank attracts immediate attention from bank tellers and bank management. The Feds have strict rules for reporting such deposits. It's a trap designed to snare drug dealers laundering cash or depositors moving cash around to fool the IRS. But it also snared innocent depositors.

If I kept it in my apartment the cops would find it. Same for my pickup truck.

A thought struck me. I wadded the bills together into one pack, wrapped them in grocery shopping bags and tucked the package in my pocket. I waited until about 10 p.m., locked my apartment and walked down three flights of stairs to the laundry room in the building's basement. Most of the ladies in the apartment building gathered in the laundry room on Saturday or Sunday mornings or early evenings after work to wash and gossip. I normally did a wash late at night to avoid gabbing with nosy neighbors, so I knew the laundry room would be deserted.

I switched on the overhead neon lights, walked past the washers and dryers and opened the door to the closet-sized room where the janitor kept his cleaning supplies. I once searched it while looking for bleach for my wash. I didn't find any bleach but did notice some old loose bricks in a recess of the wall behind the mops at floor level.

I pushed the mops aside, got down on my knees, and gently removed the loose bricks. Then carefully inserted the package of bills into the empty space behind them, replaced the bricks and covered them with mops and cleaning rags. The money would be safe there until I needed it for living expenses.

Nobody, except the janitor, had any need to enter the closet, and I didn't think he would be a problem. I had caught him napping in the basement a couple of times with the strong smell of alcohol surrounding him. His curiosity didn't range much beyond sipping cheap whiskey and finding a place to snooze.

I returned to my apartment, buoyed somewhat by having bought myself some breathing room. The unexpected windfall would keep me afloat until I found a new job courtesy of C-Level Careers America. My financial problems should then evaporate as quickly as morning fog on a bright, hot summer day. Perhaps, at some future date, I could return the money. But even as the thought entered my mind, I knew it would never happen. I had already crossed the threshold from law abiding citizen to felonious criminal just as my old man had. Or, as my mom would say, from virtue to iniquity. There was no return. The deed had already been done.

My only salvation was to swear never again to succumb to the temptation to commit a criminal act. I crossed myself and pledged never again to steal.

I wasn't the religious type, hadn't been to church since high school, but Catholic indoctrination from my early years took hold. I dropped to my knees and silently thanked God for helping me. Until it came to me that God wasn't particularly anxious to answer the prayers of thieves.

TEN

Let me tell you about Atlanta, a city of stark contrasts. Of eight-lane highways and clogged traffic, of million-dollar homes and rundown shacks, of world-class universities and failing Atlanta public schools, of downscale Walmart stores and upscale Neiman Marcus stores, of high culture and pop culture, of racial progress and KKK recruitment drives, of rednecks and sophisticates, of high crime city streets and low crime suburbia.

Most of all, Atlanta is a thriving business community. From large companies like Coca-Cola and Delta Airlines to the literally thousands of small companies and mom and pop retail stores, business is the name of the game in Atlanta. It's what makes the city come alive and what makes it flourish.

~ ~ ~

It was a late Tuesday afternoon. I had rushed over from Mackles after my shift, and was now sitting in the office of one such business in the upscale Buckhead business district. Specifically, the offices of C-Level Careers America. Trace Andrews, one of the firm's vice-presidents assigned to work with me individually to design my job campaign, closed his office door, sat down behind his desk and swiveled his executive chair around to face me. His face lit up in a smile of welcome.

"Sam, great to have you aboard as a client."

Trace was in his fifties, well-groomed and dressed in a dark blue business suit. Like Rex Hanover, his boss, he radiated confidence and looked every part the chief executive. An appropriate persona for a career consultant dealing with executive job candidates.

"Thanks, Trace. I'm looking forward to your help. God knows, I need it."

Trace winked at me and cupped his hands as seen in the Allstate commercial on TV. "You're in good hands at C-Level Careers America."

I chuckled. It was comforting to hear, but I couldn't help thinking that Trace and Rex and the other three vice presidents of C-Level Careers America looked and behaved like cookie cutter clones. Same age, same athletic physique, same graying hair, same Brooks Brothers business suits, same striped ties, same glistening black lace-up shoes, same salesman chatter, same insincere smiles and good cheer, same everything.

Then I scolded myself and chased that nasty thought from my head. Mom, who was a fountain of pieties, would have wagged her finger at me. *Be grateful for the help of people, whoever they might be. Don't turn you back on them.* Good advice but, at seventeen I had a cocky, don't give a shit attitude that I didn't grow out of for years.

Not anymore. I wanted *to* kick myself in the ass. *Why all of a sudden these bad thoughts? I should consider myself lucky to receive the kind of professional help Rex and Trace offered ... regardless of the cost. It was precisely the expert guidance I needed.*

"What did you think of the seminar, Sam?"

"I liked it. A good introduction to job hunting essentials."

The C-Level seminar, conducted the previous weekend, gathered the latest group of clients who had bought the C-Level Careers America program, to instruct them in the fundamentals of networking contacts, resume preparation, interviewing style and negotiating salary and benefits packages.

Job seekers, all, including me. The class had 15 men and three women. By my assessment, all but four clients were in their fifties, and maybe one or two in their early sixties.

The older clients had an air of desperation about them, and it showed. It came from their haunted eyes, their shaking hands, their trembling lips. It was scary and pitiful. And it shook me. During a break in the seminar I examined my face in a bathroom mirror. Was I one of them? After all, I was in my fifties and out of work and running out of money. Did my desperation show? My hands didn't tremble and my hands didn't shake, and I knew I presented a good front.

But my eyes. Did they give me away? Did they reveal my true state of anxiety? I wasn't sure.

Trace leaned forward. "Are you okay, Sam?"

I took a deep breath and composed myself. "Sure, no problem, Trace. Sorry, but my mother passed away recently, and I haven't fully recovered emotionally." That was a blatant lie, but I had to provide some excuse for my inattentiveness.

Trace, ever solicitous, came from behind his desk

to sit in a chair next to me and gently pat my back. "I know what you're going through, Sam. My Dad died last year and it tore me up."

Trace glanced out the window and his brow furrowed. He had tears in his eyes. I know this is unkind but I wondered if Trace was being sincere or if the tears were a put-on by an accomplished actor. Since getting the boot from Bowkart, my outlook on life and work had turned cynical.

Trace blew his nose and rose from his chair. "Tell you, what, Sam, let's get started. This week I'll draft your resume and cover letters, and we'll discuss how you can develop your network of contacts."

I know I showed my dismay. "I've already exhausted any job contacts I had."

Trace waved his hands in dismissal. "I'll show you how to develop a new list. Trust me."

We went on with the first session, and I was grateful for the new ideas Trace suggested, but inside, my guts were churning. *Would Mackles management find out that I had stolen $7500 from the payroll office?*

~ ~ ~

After the fire, Mackles shut down the warehouse for three days until it could cleanup enough to re-start pick and pack and shipping operations. The only damage to hardware products in the bins had been from oily smoke residue. The building itself remained intact. The warehouse crew, myself included, were given rags soaked in a mild alkali detergent to clean the parts as we picked them from bins. It stunk like hell and made me gag several times. The company supplied masks for all of us, but wearing them made breathing difficult, so few wore them, including me.

On the second day back, in the middle of my shift cleaning parts, I was called to the front office. When I arrived, the warehouse supervisor had a shit-eating grin splattered across his face. "Your turn in the barrel, O'Hara." He pointed to a glass enclosed office. "That's where you go. Now!"

The bastard didn't like me, never had since my first day, resented my white-collar background and took particular pleasure in berating me.

The word had gotten out the day before about an investigation into the cause of the fire. But I suspected there was more to it than a fire. Specifically, the missing $7500.

The grapevine had it that Mackles management hired a private investigation firm to grill any and all employees who had access to the payroll office the day of the fire. All of us were scheduled for interviews, along with office staff. Today was the day.

I looked inside the office and my heart jumped into overdrive. A bald guy the size of a small truck, squeezed into a shabby business suit, sat behind a desk. The flesh from his neck spilled over his shirt collar. He looked like a thug dressed for the execution. My execution.

He beckoned me to enter. I did and stood until he signaled me to take the lone chair directly opposite him in front of his desk.

I sat down and stole a few looks at him. The wrinkles and creases in his face told me he had weathered a thousand storms. His eyes were like two black coals plucked directly from the fires of hell. At least they looked that way in my highly anxious state.

He neither smiled nor scowled. Just sat there and froze me with a withering stare. I looked away and cleared my throat. A minute or so ticked by. It felt like an hour.

"Nervous, are you?" He had a faint Irish accent.

"No, not at all."

A skeptical grin crept along the sides of his mouth. He held up a file with hands the size of swollen heads of lettuce. The knuckles on both hands were scarred. "This is your file. Guess what's in it."

"I don't know."

"Says here you were a purchasing agent. That right?"

I cleared my throat again. "Yes, it is."

"I know all about purchasing agents. I come across those crooks all the time."

I sat there dumbfounded, and gripped the arms of my chair. I started to break out in a sweat. Baldy noticed it and sneered.

"Purchasing agents." Baldy mocked. "In my opinion, at one time or another they *all* get paid off by vendors."

I sat straight up in my chair and glared at Baldy. "I never took money from vendors."

"Yeah, I'll bet," he said, sneering. "How about paid vacations in the Caribbean, Titleist golf clubs, sixty-inch TVs, those kind of goodies?"

"That's not me, you're talking about. That's someone else." I thought my heart would explode. I squeezed the seat of my chair so hard I was afraid I would sprain my hands.

Baldy played the staring game again. I was beginning to understand that putting me on the defensive was his way of sweating out a confession. Must have been a cop in his previous life.

"Let's talk about the day of the fire. Tell me where you were and what happened."

I tried to keep my voice from trembling as I told him where I was and what I did the day of the fire.

"Did you go by the payroll office to collect your pay?"

Here it comes. Did I collect my pay? Tricky bastard. "Are you kidding? I'm paid by the temp agency that got me this job. All I wanted to do was get the hell out of the building. Like everybody else, I raced for the nearest exit."

The sneers and withering stare again. "So, you're telling me you didn't even go near the payroll office?"

"Look, I was in a near panic. I just wanted to get out of the building. I ran down the office corridor. Didn't look left or right. Just got the hell out."

The stare again. "Okay, O'Hara, that's all for now."

I got to my feet and walked as calmly as I could out of his office, down the hall and into the nearest men's room. I opened a stall and sat down on a toilet seat and started shaking like the limbs of a small tree in a hurricane.

If Baldy had suspected I had anything to do with the payroll theft I would have already been in handcuffs. I breathed a sigh of relief and kept my fingers crossed.

It wasn't until fifteen minutes later that I found my legs and returned to the job.

~ ~ ~

Three days later Mackles laid-off the entire pick and pack crew as well as some office employees. Nothing was ever mentioned about the payroll theft. My guess was Mackles management couldn't finger who had committed the crime, and decided to get rid of all of us. Another better safe than sorry management decision.

I should have felt guilty. My crime resulted in many employees losing their jobs. Somehow, it didn't affect me. Yes, I felt sorry for them, but deep down I secretly rejoiced in the success of my crime. I had fooled Mackles management and that bald-headed son-of-a-bitch who questioned me. My spirits soared. It felt extra good considering that it was another executive team, this one from Bowkart Industries, USA, that had kicked me to the street and never gave a good shit about it. Poor man's revenge, but how I reveled it. For the first time in about a year my face wasn't dragging on the ground.

Then another kick in the teeth. The temporary employment firm that hired me fired me the same day Mackles laid me off. Like Mackles, they couldn't take the chance that one of their temp employees had been responsible for the theft.

Yes, it was my fault, but when you're a couple of steps away from living underneath a bridge, you're not thinking of other people. You're thinking of survival.

ELEVEN

Maralita was lying on her stomach, stretched out next to me on my bed.

"I don't know if I ever told you," I said, "but you have a really cute ass for a thirty-eight-year old." She was also cute elsewhere, all 5'3", 110 pounds of her, yummy cocoa complexion, pert nose and curly brown hair included.

She reached over and gently slapped my hand. "Is sex all you think about?"

"I think about you all the time."

She rolled over and snuggled up to me and kissed me. "I think about you all the time, too, querida mia."

My darling. Warm and delightful words from a lovely lady. She often spoke such words and phrases to me in Spanish, her native tongue. Maralita was Mexican-American, her parents from Monterrey, Mexico, where her father had worked as an engineer for Carrier Corporation. When he was transferred to Carrier operations in Indianapolis, Maralita's family emigrated to the USA and eventually became American citizens. Unfortunately for Maralita, her parents died in a car wreck after attending a New Year's Eve party. She had been an English major in college, but with the death of her parents and no regular income to count on, she quit in her junior year, on her own at twenty, her story quite similar to mine.

Maralita bounced around for several years, working at whatever job she could find until she ran out of her small inheritance. She lived in a flurry of cities, looking for work, looking for love, looking for stability, but not really finding anything or anybody she could anchor to. Her dismal work prospects kept her on the move and one step above the poverty line.

Finally, a bright spot. She landed a job as flight attendant for a Mexican airline that flew routinely between Mexican vacation destinations and the southern American states. Atlanta was its American hub.

Her boyfriend at the time was a member of the Sinaloa drug cartel who traveled frequently to the States. Since the Mexican airline paid its employees slave wages, her boyfriend persuaded her to supplement her paltry income by smuggling drug-money dollars from the USA to Mexico. She reluctantly agreed, her options few. Mexican women in the States worked at mostly low-paying menial jobs, and high-paying jobs in Mexico were hard to come by for women.

On her second trip from Atlanta to Puerto Vallarta, Mexico, Maralita was stopped by US Customs with a bag full of one-hundred dollar bills in a hidden compartment, about one million dollars in total. She was arrested, jailed and tried swiftly, the money confiscated by the USA government. Since this was her first offense, she received a five-year sentence and was released on parole after serving two years and two months.

Maralita had an apartment in the same dismal

building where I lived. I met her by accident in the street in front of our apartment building when her twelve-year-old Honda Civic broke down and she urgently needed a lift to her parole officer. Lucky for her, I happened to be parked close by. Terrified that she would be late for her appointment, violate her parole and get sent back to federal prison, she practically begged me for a lift. That's how I met her.

"When do your job hunting classes start?" she asked me.

"They've already started. Thank God. Keep your fingers crossed that I land something soon."

"That man you told me about, the one who promised you a job. That sounds phony. Is he for real?"

"I'm counting on it."

"Look, querida, I don't know this man, this Rex Hanover you told me about, but I don't like the way his company sounds."

I pulled back and looked at her. "It's my only choice. Either he finds something for me or I start living under a bridge, homeless."

Maralita had a hard edge to her. She was suspicious of everything and everybody. I wrote that off to her three plus years in prison. I supposed that terrifying experience was enough to make anybody distrustful.

Just the opposite defined me. I didn't have that same hard edge as Maralita. My life until the recent layoff from Bowkart Industries had not been stressful, not anywhere in the sense that Maralita's life was. Perhaps not having to fight to survive, like most

Americans perched on the financial edge of ruin, made me too easy-going and soft.

She held me in her arms. "I know you'll be successful, querida. I have faith in you."

"If I'm not, you'll have to take care of me," I said half-humorously. Maralita had a job as a room maid at a Buckhead Marriott. There was no way her pitiful wage was going to support me. Even if she could, I wouldn't allow it.

"Let's say that if things get really bad, querida, I know a way out ... for both of us."

I gave her a funny look but she burrowed her face into my neck and I decided to let it go for now. *What way out?*

~ ~ ~

I was back on the street again, hustling for jobs, calling and recalling every contact from my old Rolodex, until their secretaries and assistants started ignoring, then blocking, my phone calls. Employment agencies offered nothing now they hadn't offered before when I first started looking for a job. Which was either "sorry, no jobs available," or slim pickings work like fast food, and I swore I would never return to slinging fries, working alongside 17-year-olds.

My once a week meetings with Trace Andrews at C-Level Careers America continued but yielded absolutely nothing. Trace used his "exclusive" executive database to help me select top level management people to contact. That so-called exclusive database was straight out of Standard and Poor's. What a rip-off! I paid eight grand when I could have gotten the same information free from the nearest public library.

Still, I followed Trace's instructions, sent out a couple of hundred resumes, had a few desultory conversations with executive assistants, but nothing came from it. Not one single in-person interview. The job market for white-collar workers had shrunk dramatically, and top management posts were being filled by executives with extensive experience in general management, not specialists like me. Another phony C-Level Careers America promise of companies seeking executives from the ranks that turned out to be deceptive.

Rex Hanover's commitment to find a job for me within 90 was far behind schedule. In plain terms, his promises didn't amount to shit. We were now close to 120 days without a single valid lead in my job hunt. I smelled a rat. It was finally dawning on me that I had been conned.

What to do next? I knew that whatever it was, I better do it fast. My small cash hoard was rapidly depleting with no prospects for replenishment on the horizon. In retrospect, if I hadn't stolen $7500 from Mackles I would right now be flat broke and homeless. Maybe that was God's way to tide me over until I found legitimate work. I silently prayed for His help, knowing fully that I was still asking Him to condone my immoral behavior. Shameless, I know, but I was desperate, and desperate men and women cling to the tiniest shred of hope.

~ ~ ~

Just how legitimate was C-Level Careers America? Hell of a time to inquire, considering that I had already handed over most of what little money I had, but I decided to find out, anyway.

First thing I did was check the company online.

The C-Level Careers America website was chock full of endorsements from former clients. Reading them, you would think Rex Hanover had fulfilled all of his clients' lifelong dreams and all of them were now happily residing in executive suites across the country. But I knew that wasn't true. Other members of my class were grumbling, too, expressing the same doubts I had. According to them, this exercise in finding meaningful work was turning into a mirage of disappointments.

From the website's endorsements, I randomly selected 10 names and called every one of those names in the phone book, no matter how many times their names appeared. For example, the phone book listed five Alice Jones. I called all five but didn't find any clients of C-Level Careers America. Same story for the other nine names I selected. Not a one of those folks I reached had even heard of C-Level Careers America. At the end of the calls, my fingers were numb and I was left with the same feeling as Hamlet's sentry Marcellus when he tells his boss, "Something is rotten in the state of Denmark." Sure, all 10 of those former clients could have moved out of state, but that was highly unlikely. Not all 10.

While researching online I came across a few newspaper articles in *The Atlanta Journal-Constitution* describing lawsuits former clients had launched against C-Level Careers America. Every one of those articles had been written by an investigative reporter for the newspaper named Ron Lonquist. I called him at his office in the newspaper, told him my story and he suggested that we meet after working hours for a drink and discussion at George's, a local no-frills pub in downtown Atlanta frequented by serious drinkers.

I showed up at 5:30 p.m. The pub was so dark it could have been an underground cave. I'm not much of a boozer anymore but I know several people who are serious drinkers and they seem to prefer darkness and solitude while they pay homage to alcohol.

I waited a couple of minutes until my eyes acclimated to the dark, then looked around for Lonquist. He saw me first and signaled me to come to his booth in the back of the room.

"How'd you know what I look like?" I asked Lonquist as I sat down across from him.

"I don't. But you looked out of place as soon as you entered the bar. This is a newspaper bar, after-work home of half of The *Journal-Constitution*'s staff. You don't fit the image."

Lonquist looked like a newspaper reporter from a fifties movie. Disheveled brown hair, suit jacket off, tie loosened, sleeves rolled up his arms, a drink in his hands, a cigarette dangling from his lips. A scowl on his lips. He got right to the point: "You got stung by Rex Hanover. How much did he take you for?"

I shook my head slowly. "Eight grand, and another four grand if and when he finds me an executive position."

Lonquist sucked on his cigarette and nodded. "That's maybe slightly more than average."

I batted the smoke away and raised my eyebrows. "How much is average?"

Lonquist stubbed out his cigarette and waved the smoke away. "Sorry." He signaled the waitress over and ordered a double scotch. "What are you having?"

"Draft beer. Hey, the rounds are on me."

"Get the next one." Lonquist stared at the waitress' ample bosom. She winked at Lonquist and said, "Like the merchandise, Ron?"

"Love it, Mandy."

The waitress walked away, and Lonquist said, "Sam, as far as I can tell, the average scam is about five to seven grand. But I have seen it go as high as twenty-thousand."

I whistled. "How do they get away with it?"

Lonquist sighed. "Most of the people who use services from con artist firms like C-Level Careers America are out of work, out of money and out of time. Many have been out of work for three or four years and they've lost confidence in themselves. When a smooth-talking hustler like Rex Hanover comes along they bite and bite hard and hand over whatever money they have left. Some even borrow money to hand over to phonies like Rex Hanover."

What he said stung. I think my silence spoke loud and clear.

"Look," Lonquist said, "I'm talking in generalities, not specifically about you, so don't feel bad."

"I can handle it."

"You're not alone. You've got lots and lots of company. Some pretty smart guys and gals got taken. Considering all of the career marketing scams in

Atlanta alone, I would say a couple of thousand unemployed work white-collar workers in the area have been ripped-off by swindlers like Rex Hanover and his gang of cutthroats."

The waitress returned with our drinks. Lonquist's eyes never wandered far from Mandy's bosom.

After she left, I said, "How successful are career firms like C-Level Careers America in finding jobs for their clients? What percent of them actually find jobs?"

Lonquist sat back in the booth and thought about it for a minute. "That's hard to pin down, because those bastards will never give you the straight skinny. In fact, all career marketing firms exaggerate the number of their success stories. But I'll venture a guess and say maybe 25 percent."

That shocked me. "Twenty-five percent? How can they even stay in business?"

"Because the truth is hidden, and they prey on innocent, unsuspecting clients. Even when angry clients take them to court, Rex and his gang always come out on top."

"Do a lot of clients sue them? I've been thinking along those lines myself."

Lonquist snorted, then threw down one of his double scotches while I sipped my beer.

"Don't waste your time and money. Sharks like Hanover have a pair of bloodthirsty lawyers they use in court. Those guys are fucking vicious. They'll lie and submit phony documents which show how inattentive you've been –"

I almost choked on my beer. "Inattentive?" That's

a crock of shit. I've been busting my balls to follow the program."

Lonquist smiled ruefully. "I'm sure you have, and so do most of the others, but the guy who helped you develop your job approach – a vice president in your case – will testify that he could barely keep you awake."

"But that's a lie!"

Lonquist sat back in the booth and sighed. "Welcome to the world of career marketing. And a further welcome to shit-out-of-luck city. You've been had."

~ ~ ~

The following morning I entered the C-Level Careers America lobby about 10:00a.m. and told the receptionist I wanted to talk with Rex Hanover. I was angry and didn't try to hide it. She called Rex's office. After a couple of minutes on the phone, she hung up and with a frosty voice told me Rex was busy. I got the feeling that she had been through this many times before and that Rex wasn't busy but simply trying to avoid me.

I spun around and walked down the hall to Trace Andrew's office and told him about my conversation with Ron Longuist. He turned pale and asked me to have a seat, then left his office and returned five minutes later with Elaine Dayton in tow.

"You're the lady I talked with on the phone. You set up my appointment with Rex."

Elaine's melodious voice on the phone didn't match the iciness of her voice in person. She reminded me of my mean-spirited third grade teacher, a lady who enjoyed slapping her students' knuckles with a ruler. "How may I be of service to you, Mr. O'Hara?"

"Rex promised to get me a job in 90 days. It hasn't happened. No interviews, no offers, just plain nothing, except for eight thousand I forked over to enrich the coffers of your firm."

Trace started to speak but Elaine cut him off. "I'll handle this, Trace." The coldness in her voice dipped from freezing to thirty below and her eyes shot cold darts at me. "You'll just have to continue on with your program, Mr. O'Hara. Trace will help you."

"But –"

"If you review your contract and what Mr. Hanover said, you will find that he did not guarantee to find you a job, only that he would do the best he could to help you find one."

I felt the color drain from my face. "That's a lie. It's bullshit. He promised me."

She paled. "We don't tolerate that kind of language in this firm." She picked up her cell phone and called somebody named Wilbur. Within 60 seconds Wilbur showed up as I stood there shaking in anger and disbelief while Elaine Dayton coldly ignored me, and Trace cringed.

Wilbur, a black guy, stood about 6'6" and packed what looked like 300 pounds of muscle. He had a friendly look but the way he gripped my arm and led me to the back door, away from the reception area of the firm, told me he wasn't friendly at all. He tossed me into the hallway and slammed the door behind him. I left the building feeling the same way I did in

No Jobs Available

Marine boot camp when my platoon was deprived a weekend off because a recruit dropped his rifle, a sin to end all sins in the Marine Corps. We called it feeling depressed, dejected and fucked up. Just like now. Eight grand down the tubes. Bastards!

That was the last I ever heard of C-Level Careers America.

TWELVE

Nobody in his right mind wants to stand alone. Nobody except a recluse or a nut case. The point is that man does not live by bread alone. He needs that one special woman, not only for sex, although without it, let's face it, the average guy tends to become excessively aggressive, but also for a sweetheart who will listen to his gripes and complaints and comfort him. Some understanding, supportive woman he can turn to in times of stress. For me, that woman was Maralita.

She had knocked on my apartment door one evening a couple of days after I gave her a lift to the parole office. She carried with her a tray of sugarless cookies to thank me for rescuing her from a possible parole violation (During our car trip to her parole officer I mentioned that I was diabetic). I ate a cookie or two and we talked over Diet Cokes as she told me her story. In return I told her mine. Our accounts were predictably similar: two drifters at the lower rung of the economic ladder, barely scraping along, struggling to survive, both fighting to keep from living in the street. Her situation more acute than mine because she was an ex-con. We put our heads together and struggled to find a solution, a way out of this mess.

I wondered how many other couples were sitting at their kitchen tables discussing how they could avoid being thrown out of their homes for missed rental or mortgage payments. Or how many of them skimped on groceries. Or how many of them couldn't scrape together enough money to pay for their kids' school clothing. The thought of all that misery made me boil over with anger. What was wrong with our country that so many people existed on the fringe? We were rich compared to most other countries, and had a vast number of resources. Didn't make sense. I took several deep breaths to calm myself.

Maralita squeezed my hand and I squeezed back. Before long a recognition of mutual circumstance and need and attraction took hold and led us into the bedroom. The lovemaking helped restore my wounded spirits. We were in our own private world, two lonely and frightened people consoling each other, the sex and loving reminding us, that while down and almost out, we were still human beings. That's how our relationship started.

~ ~ ~

After getting booted from the C-Level Careers America office I went directly to Maralita's apartment in a near panic. It was her day off, and she was preparing a sandwich for lunch.

"Querida, what's wrong?"

I collapsed into a chair at her kitchen table. "Right now, all I want is a drink."

Maralita looked at me with alarm, stopped what she was doing and came over to me and rubbed the back of my neck. "Are you okay?"

"No, I'm not." I told her about getting kicked out of the C-Level Careers America office. She sat on my lap and we put our arms around each other. "It's going to be okay," she crooned. "I know it is. "We can face this together."

"I got swindled."

"Can you take them to court? Make them pay back the money they took from you?"

I told her about Lonquist and how he said a lawsuit would be a huge waste of time and money. "Problem is, Maralita, I'm shit out of luck. I've got enough money to last another few weeks, that's it."

It was true. In the four months since meeting Maralita I had gone through most of the $7500 I'd stashed away in the laundry room of my apartment building and had about $800 left. That, and my small food stamp allotment, and free insulin shots at the public health center, were all I had to my name.

"You can live with me, in my apartment. We'll make out."

"Not for long, and not like this. You know better."

We clung to each other, kindred spirits locked in the same anguish of poverty, urgently seeking a way out. Not knowing where to turn next. At least I didn't know where to turn next. Apparently, Maralita did.

She sat up and placed her hands on my cheeks and locked eyes with me. "There are other ways to make a living."

I snorted. "Like rob a bank?"

She placed a fingertip on my mouth. "Hush, querida." She rose and walked over to a kitchen cabinet and took out an unopened fifth of Chivas Regal scotch. "I've been saving this bottle for a special occasion such as today."

I suppressed a laugh of disbelief. "What's so special about today?"

She handed the scotch to me. There was a glint in her eyes. While I opened the bottle, she said with great deliberation, "Because today is the beginning of a new life for you, for me, for both of us together, querida."

"I don't get it. Beginning of what?"

"I know how we can make a small fortune."

I glanced at her eyes. They were full of promise and resolve.

~ ~ ~

"Don't keep me in suspense," I said. "What are you talking about?"

Maralita took the bottle of Chivas Regal from me and sat down on a chair opposite mine at the kitchen table. She poured us each a drink. "First, drink up. It will help settle you down."

"Down the hatch," I said. I threw my head back and downed the drink. Maralita followed suit. We both choked, eyes tearing, then laughed.

"Not too tough, are we? Not like Sam Spade, the private eye who could handle his booze. That's for sure."

Maralita looked puzzled. "Sam Spade ..."

I explained who Sam Spade was. "The tough fictional detective who could throw shot after shot of booze down his throat without blinking, then go out and solve a crime. The guy's an American institution."

We took another drink, this time sipping it. The scotch helped relax me, as Maralita promised. "Now, go ahead and tell me how we're going to become rich."

"You may not like this. It's illegal."

That stopped me cold. I had already committed a crime and I shuddered when I thought of topping that with yet another crime. But my curiosity was aroused, and I had to admit a small fortune sounded good, very good, considering my future prospects were in the tank. "Let's hear it, anyway."

"There's a lot money available to people who are willing to mule drugs and money."

"By mule, you mean smuggle?"

"Exactly."

I threw my hands up. "Whoa, that's craziness. Between the Border Patrol and DEA[3], we don't stand a chance. Hell, Maralita, you got caught right here in Atlanta smuggling money before you even set foot on a plane."

Maralita shrugged. "Querida, I'm not talking about carrying money across the border. Yes, it's risky, and the last thing I want is to serve more time in prison. It was the worst two years of my life."

"If not the border, where else are you talking about?"

Maralita's eyes gleamed. "Moving money within the borders of the United States."

"I'm not with you. I'm assuming the drugs come from Mexico or somewhere else in Central or South America."

Maralita said they do.

"Then the money has to be smuggled back to the

---

[3] Drug Enforcement Agency

same place the drugs came from, correct?"

"That's the beauty of this. It has to be smuggled back across the border to Mexico, but not by us. All we have to do is pick up payments at a few different places across the country from major drug distributors and deliver them to a contact in Las Cruces, New Mexico. That's it. Nothing else."

"Let me get this straight. What we would be doing is collecting money for drugs smuggled into the country. Is that right?"

"Yes."

"How does the money get back to Mexico?"

"Somebody else in New Mexico flies it over in a small private plane. But we're not involved with that."

I stopped questioning Maralita for a moment and stared at her. "Where did you learn how this works, Maralita? You never collected money from drug distributors in the States, did you?"

Maralita shook her head no. "An older American couple gathered the money from American drug distributors in different locations around the country and drove it to Gilberto in Atlanta. He gave me the suitcase with the hidden compartment and packed it with the money. I got caught on my second trip from Atlanta to Puerto Vallarta."

"Gilberto?"

Her eyes danced away from mine. "My boyfriend at the time."

"Oh, I see," I said with a little surprise and frost mixed in my voice.

"Stop acting foolishly, Sam. I haven't seen Gilberto in years." When Maralita was angry or upset with me, she called me Sam, not querida or querida mia.

I did feel foolish. "Tell me about the older couple. How did they get in the act?"

"They were an old married couple in their late sixties who needed the money Gilberto paid them. He thought they would be less suspect than a younger person or a younger couple, and less likely to be stopped by the police."

"Makes sense. But where does that leave us, and why isn't Gilberto using the same older couple?"

"They called it quits after a couple of runs. Ran out of nerve. And, let's face it, they're not a young or even middle-age couple."

"So, we make one run across the States, driving to the pickup point and deliver the money to some other person in Las Cruces, New Mexico. Why not fly?"

"Gilberto stopped using public airlines after my capture. Too much of a chance to get caught."

"Let me get this straight. We get a car and pickup drug money from drug distributors and deliver it. All within the country. That's all, nothing else?"

"And from drug dealers, too."

"Okay. And drug dealers. I don't know the lingo. But I want to make sure we don't have to do this for the rest of our lives."

Maralita's eyelids flickered. "There might be another run."

I knew I would be on edge the entire time we carried large sums of money in a car for thousands of miles. I'm not a career criminal and didn't have the chutzpah of those engaged in the drug trade. To make matters worse, the DEA and cops chase drug dealers and distributors and we might cross their path.

"Two runs might be okay, but I want to stop after that. Then we go somewhere fresh where we both can start over."

She shrugged. "That's simple. We just tell Gilberto two runs is all we do."

"I'm assuming Gilberto will supply us with the car."

"Yes, along with expense money and phony credit cards. Oh yeah, fake passports, too, in case we need to leave the country suddenly."

"Phony passports and credit cards? How does that work?"

"We use a fake card at each stop we make for hotels and restaurants, shred it afterward, and use a different one for the next collection point."

"Where does he get the credit cards and passports?"

Maralita heaved a sigh. "Gilberto's a criminal. He has his sources. He's part of a large Mexican cartel. They can buy any service they want."

"Is Gilberto Mexican or American?"

"He was born in Mexico and raised in the States. In Los Angeles. But he works for the cartel."

"Then they own him."

Maralita gave me a funny look. "He has an associate's college degree."

I guffawed. "Big deal. Okay, he's an educated gangster."

Maralita's face reddened. She clamped her jaw shut. "Hey, I wasn't talking about you."

The anger in Maralita's face told me I had stepped over the line. "Look, everything I know about Mexican cartels scares the hell out of me."

"Don't let it. Believe me, all they want is to get the money across the border into their hands. These are businessmen."

"Say we made one run across the country and brought the money to Las Cruces. How much money would Gilberto pay us?"

Maralita poured us another drink. Her eyes sparkled. "He will pay us 50,000 dollars, querida. Fifty-thousand dollars for each run."

"That's a lot." I leaned back in my chair. Visions of stacked one-hundred dollar bills and what they would buy danced in my head like sugar plums.

"How much drug money will we carry in the car?"

"One. maybe two million."

I clicked my tongue. "Wow! That much money makes us a target, a *big* target. It's kind of scary, carrying that much money around."

Maralita chuckled. "We're not going to carry the money in plain sight, querida. There are ways to hide it."

"I don't know about this. I just don't know."

Maralita squeezed my hand as if holding on to a lifeline. "It's how we get to live like humans again, querida, instead of like dogs."

I held her close to me. "You said we could live together in your apartment and do okay."

"Querida, I wanted to let you know you've got someplace to live in case the bottom falls out. But living poor is not okay. Not really. That's existing, not living."

"It's just that ... well, the risk is so high."

"I don't care. I want my life back, the one I had before I went to prison. I want to live well, not in squalor. And I know you want it too."

I saw the determination in her eyes, felt it in the grip of her hand.

"I'll do anything to get it back. Will you join me, querida?'

I looked deep inside her eyes. In that moment our souls, our lives, our destiny connected. I kissed her. "Yes, my love. I will join you. I love you very much."

"Querida, te amo muchisimo, tambien." I love you very much, too.

We hugged for a few moments. Then she stepped back. There was fire in her eyes. "But first, we must get approval from Hector."

THIRTEEN

Gilberto was waiting for us when we disembarked from the Mexican air flight in Culiacan, a large city in the state of Sinaloa, Mexico. He was older than I imagined, maybe around late forties, with curly gray hair and creases that cut through his face like knife wounds.

He kissed Maralita on both of her cheeks. "Glad you made it okay in prison," was all he said to her. He scowled at me. "You're the lover boy, eh?"

I didn't like his wise guy attitude, but if we were going to work together I needed his help. It wouldn't pay to cross him and get our relationship off to a rocky start. I was also acutely aware of the vicious reputation of Mexican cartel members hit men, called sicarios, who routinely kill to protect the cartel's turf and drugs. I reminded myself that I was in a dangerous country.

I held Maralita's hand and said, "Thanks for inviting us, Gilberto."

He grunted an acknowledgement. He had a stone face that revealed no emotion beyond the few words spilling grudgingly out of his mouth and his apparent contempt for me.

I watched Maralita carefully to see if there was any magic left between her and Gilberto, but detected nothing.

Gilberto signaled to Mexican customs agents and

we bypassed customs and the necessity of showing them our passports. Such is the power of the Sinaloa drug cartel.

"Come, we go now. I have a car waiting at the curb. Any checked baggage?"

We both said no and strode with him through the airport to the arrival entrance. A black Ford Explorer sat at the curb. The driver rushed out of the car and opened the rear door for us. Gilberto issued instructions to him and we drove off.

The top honcho in the Sinaloa cartel had insisted on taking a look at me before allowing both Maralita and me to transport money for the cartel. Not a bad business decision. You always want to know who you're dealing with.

We drove about thirty minutes or so through the city and into hills above Culiacan. Gilberto was silent throughout the ride and Maralita and I said nothing, just looked out the car windows at the lush tropical landscape.

Near the top of one hill we approached a gate attached to a 15-foot-high steel mesh fence. The fence extended in both directions through the tree line as far as I could see. The driver punched in a code at the entry kiosk and the gate swung open and closed behind us. The Ford shifted into a lower gear and we climbed a steep hill until we came upon a clearing that extended over 100 yards in front of the house. I remembered my Marine Corps tactical training: This long visible approach was a smart way to alert the house's inhabitants of approaching trouble.

The house itself was really a mansion. It was

made from cut limestone, stood two stories high, about a half-block wide, and was as large and resplendent as a luxury hotel. I noticed a tennis court around the side of the house, adjacent to an Olympic-size swimming pool. Several children shouted and chased one another around the pool playing Marco Polo. Their gleeful, carefree voices floated to us in the afternoon air.

The Ford dropped us off at the grand entrance. And grand it was with a ten-foot-high mahogany door flanked by fluted mahogany columns that rose twenty feet into a portico roof.

A guard stood in front of the house holding an

AK-47. Another guard about 10 yards away held a vicious-looking M-16 grenade launcher. Both guards looked at us as if they were hunters and we were dinner and they were hungry.

The front door swung open and a tall, broad shouldered man dressed in expensive casual wear strolled out to greet us. His friendly face was wreathed in smiles.

He shook hands with me as if I were a long-lost friend. "Mr. O'Hara, welcome to my home. My name is Hector. So nice of you and Maralita to accept my invitation."

Except, as interpreted by Gilberto in Atlanta, it had been more of a command.

Hector embraced Maralita. "I'm so sorry you had to endure prison. I feel responsible. How may I pay you back?"

She brushed his concern aside and Hector ushered Maralita and me through the house on a quick tour while Gilberto remained in the hallway. Along the route, he proudly pointed out a winding marble staircase with wrought-iron railings, custom-designed and handcrafted furniture – not some, but *every* piece of furniture custom-made – an imposing twenty-foot gold-leaf and crystal chandelier hanging in the foyer, hand-carved decorative wood paneling in the den and study, and original paintings of Mexican scenes by Mexican artists decorating the walls. The tour swam by in a blur of splendor designed to take our breath away.

Hector also mentioned that the house contained two elevators, an indoor tennis court, gym, and swimming pool, and an entertainment center containing a movie-house-size screen. The effect of all his wealth was overwhelming, gaudy and ostentatious, but breathtaking. Perhaps that was because of my envy. *This guy has to be richer than Bill Gates and Carlos Slim, the Mexican telecommunications magnate, combined.*

Hector led us into his study where Gilberto patiently waited. We sat down in plush, comfortable gold-embroidered chairs and chatted while a maid prepared Chinese tea and brought it to us. As we waited, I took a closer look at Hector. He hadn't told us his last name, and neither had Gilberto. But I knew it, anyway. It was Vanquez, and he was well known to both the DEA and the Mexican Federales, the country's federal police force.

Hector Vanquez was not at all like his predecessor El Chapo, a notorious drug lord, now residing in an American prison. I had expected a heavyset thug with killer's eyes, whose fierce look would make even the heartiest of men tremble. El Chapo had been the most feared man In Mexico. The hundreds of people he was accused of killing seemed to echo in the home of his successor.

But Hector looked more like a chief executive officer, more comfortable in the boardroom than behind an AK-47. His English was flawless as perhaps it should be for somebody who graduated from Princeton and earned an MBA from Harvard.

After we finished drinking our tea, Hector nodded his head at Gilberto, and Gilberto dutifully left the room.

Hector turned toward Maralita and me. "So, I hear you two want to make some money."

Maralita took the lead. "We like the arrangement, especially of working in the states, and not crossing the border."

"How about you, Sam? Are you ready for this? It could be dangerous. I say could be because if you're careful and do exactly as we instruct, you shouldn't have any problems."

"Hector, I couldn't be more ready."

He smiled and slapped the arms of his chair. "That's good news. We need exceptional people like you two. And, incidentally, working as a couple greatly reduces your chances of being stopped by law enforcement for random inspections. Smart thinking."

"When do we start?" I asked.

"As soon as you get back to the states. But first, I want to show you something interesting." He rose from his chair and said, "Please follow me."

We rode an elevator to the basement level and walked by the indoor pool and an entertainment center into the maintenance area. This large room contained a large boiler, water heaters and tanks, water pumps, backup generators, a workbench, tool racks and maintenance equipment. Obviously, in preparation for any emergency, whether man-made or natural disaster.

Hector unlocked and opened a large steel door in the back of the room and we stepped into a dimly lit chamber. He flipped a switch and bright overhead florescent lights flooded the room. After we stepped in, Hector closed and locked the door behind him.

In the center of the chamber Gilberto stood over a man who was bound to a chair and gagged. The man's eyes radiated fright. Sweat poured from his face into the gag. He muttered something indecipherable.

Hector said, "This man is an employee of my company. An unfaithful employee. He wasn't satisfied with the high wages we paid him. He felt compelled to bolster his income by informing the Federales on his associates. Because of this traitor, the Federales killed three of our men."

I caught my breath. Maralita clung to me and we stared in disbelief at the scene unfolding in front of us.

Hector turned to us. "I don't normally bring such scum into my home. I brought him here today because I want to convince you two, especially you Sam, that your loyalty to me is absolutely essential. Maralita has already demonstrated her unquestioned loyalty by going to prison without revealing Gilberto's or my identity, but now that you two are a team the equation may change. You will both be operating in the United States, away from our direct supervision, and who knows what factors may influence you. My purpose here is to convince you that any unfaithful actions will result in the most disastrous consequences."

Maralita gasped. Gilberto noticed and sneered.

"Your first wife," Hector said, talking to me, "her name is Margaret, yes? She lives now in San Diego?"

I was stunned and stood there with my mouth hung open, not understanding why Hector mentioned Margaret. *How did he even know about Margaret?*

Hector continued. "Your second wife Laura Lee, and your former associates at Bowkart ..." He stopped talking and removed a card from his shirt pocket. "Their names, Freddie Walsh who was your boss, and Donna and Charley, fellow purchasing agents." He read off their last names and placed the card back in his shirt pocket.

I felt the blood drain from my face.

"Besides you and Maralita, all these people will die if you betray me. I know where they live and work and I promise to kill them. Do you understand me, Sam?" I croaked out a yes.

Hector pushed Maralita aside, gripped my shoulders and locked eyes with me. "It's imperative you believe me." He stopped and then enunciated the following words emphatically, pausing for effect between each word: "If either you or Maralita betray me, I will kill all of you without compunction or remorse."

He stepped away from me and nodded at Gilberto. Gilberto picked up a gun from a workbench that had a silencer attached to it. The tied and gagged man's eyes bulged with fear. His cry of desperation was filtered by the gag into squeals of anguish.

Gilberto shot him twice in the back of his head. Each time it sounded like the cork popping open a bottle of champagne. Maralita and I flinched. The man tumbled over in his chair to the basement floor. His legs jerked spasmodically for a few seconds and then stopped.

My legs were so weak I thought I might collapse. Maralita covered her eyes and sobbed quietly into my chest.

Hector patted me on the back. "Nothing for you to worry about, Sam. Just remember what you saw here today. Keep it always in mind. Always."

Gilberto blew into the smoking barrel of the handgun like a gunman of the old West, and grinned at me. *This was all surreal. Had to be. This can't be happening to Sam O'Hara.*

Hector clapped his hands and smiled. "Now that this unpleasant detour is concluded, why don't we go back upstairs and have lunch." He put his arm around my shoulders as we walked. "Sam, you'll just love the teak dining room table I had imported from Indonesia."

FOURTEEN

One advantage of having money for a diabetic is being able to by insulin, which is readily available at drug stores everywhere, without resorting to a prescription. It's cheaper and you don't have to abide by insurance requirements. With expense money in my pocket, courtesy of Hector, I was able to stock up on insulin, lancets for puncturing my fingers to raise a drop of blood, and a glucose test meter for measuring my body's glucose reading. *At least I don't have to worry anymore about where my next shot of insulin is coming from. And best of all, not having to get my shot courtesy of the state government. A demeaning experience. So, at least from the money point of view, a good start to my new venture.*

We picked up our nine-year-old Chevrolet Tahoe from Gilberto in Columbia, South Carolina. The car had 110,000 miles on the odometer, but from the looks of it I would bet 200,000 miles was more like it. The sheet metal exterior was banged up and the car's interior didn't look much better.

But what this SUV had that others didn't was a hidden compartment between the rear wheel wells and trunk for hiding cash ... a mountain of it. Gilberto said we could easily carry up to two-million in fifties and hundreds. The weight of that money, maybe 50 pounds or more would not detectable in a vehicle that weighed close to 6000 pounds.

I looked under the hood. The engine looked to be in prime condition. It had a powerful souped-up V-8 engine that would be enough to burn rubber and evade either cops or thieves in a chase. Gilberto let me know that a mechanic had inspected the car and replaced components such as the battery and tires. It was ready to go.

The car was theft proof. A thief couldn't start the engine unless he entered the six-digit electronic code that only Gilberto, Maralita and I possessed. If he tried to jimmy the trunk or enter the car an alarm would sound. As a last measure, the hidden compartment was rigged with a directed explosive charge that would blow off the hands of anybody who attempted to open the secret compartment without accessing the exact code.

"Whoa," I said to Gilberto when I heard about the explosive. "Makes no sense. The bomb goes off and five minutes later cops arrive."

"The explosive charge contains black powder that will burn the money. Better that than allowing thieves to steal what rightfully belongs to us."

The concept of revenge at any cost raised goosebumps on my arms and chest. It was Hitlerian and repugnant, and frankly, it scared the hell out of me. I turned around and walked away.

Then a surprise: Maralita and I received navy-blue Salvation Army officer uniforms from Gilberto. He instructed us to wear the uniforms while driving, eating and picking up and delivering the money. In other words, anywhere in public. He told us to go online and learn everything we could about the

Salvation Army in the event that we were questioned.

The Salvation Army uniform made a lot of sense. It was a perfect cover for smuggling. If a cop stopped us, all he would see is two blessed souls doing the work of the Lord, traveling the highways to help those in need. In case the cop asked specifics, we were traveling to Salvation Army districts to assist them in setting up their summertime charity efforts.

During lunch, I took Gilberto's advice and looked up the Salvation Army online, and found many other benefits besides disguises. Businesses everywhere welcome Salvation Army soldiers of the and award them discounts on meals and motel rooms.

The old Chevrolet Tahoe fit in with our disguise. Soldiers of the Salvation Army don't travel around in BMWs or Cadillacs. That would arouse suspicion. Anybody with an ounce of knowledge about the Salvation Army realizes that its soldiers don't own or drive upscale vehicles.

Gilberto gave us the name and location of the first contact in Rhode Island where we were scheduled to pick-up our first bundle of cash, about $750,000, and deliver it to another contact in Las Cruces, New Mexico. He didn't give us the specific address of the destination nor the name of the recipient. Apparently, this was the pilot who would fly the cash over the border to Hector's people in Mexico. Gilberto said he'd let us know who and where the day before scheduled delivery.

"This should be an easy one for you," Gilberto said referring to the pickup in Rhode Island. "Your home state. You still remember your way around?"

"How'd you know where I grew up?"

Gilberto smirked. "I know everything about you."

I ignored his wise guy comment. "Yeah, I know my way around Providence and the state." I shouldn't have been surprised that Hector and Gilberto knew a lot about my background. You don't trust $750,000 to a stranger without first vetting him.

Gilberto handed over our new identities: driver's licenses from Georgia and three credit cards in fictitious names for Maralita and me. I was now Captain Johonson of the Salvation Army and Maralita was Yolanda, my wife, a soldier in the Salvation Army, both of us faithful servants of the Lord.

We thought licenses from Georgia best because we lived there and would be able to answer questions knowledgeably should we be stopped somewhere along the highway by cops.

I wanted to carry a handgun, but Gilberto turned me down. He was afraid that in something as routine as a traffic stop a cop might find the gun and arrest us and compound the car. What he said made sense from his point of view, but not from mine. Not if I wanted to protect myself if trouble erupted. I tabled the issue for now, but decided to buy a gun while on the road.

"How about our payment, the fifty grand?"

"You'll get paid when you deliver the money in Las Cruces." Instead of answering the question, Gilberto smirked, which worried me.

"Who will pay us?"

"When you arrive in Las Cruces, I'll be there to meet you." *Again, that stupid smirk. Make no mistake about it. I'll have to watch out for this son-of-a-bitch.*

Gilberto gave us our marching orders for trip expenses and behavior on the road: Denny's was in, Olive Garden was out. Motel 6 was in, the Marriott was out. No cocktail lounge evenings, no boozing. Period. At all times Maralita and I had to leave the impression of personal indigence and high moral behavior less some astute observer penetrates our cover.

"The trip, he told us, "shouldn't take more than a week. Two days to get to Providence, get the money, and four days driving to Los Cruces, New Mexico. I checked out the driving distance and time on MapQuest. I'll give you an extra day for delays along the route. It's early summer now, so there shouldn't be any weather delays. But you never know. You show up later than seven days from now, I'll know something's wrong and I'm going to come looking for you."

"How generous of you," I said.

"If you or your girlfriend get any ideas about running away with the 750 grand, just keep this in mind." He stopped and glared at me. "We won't stop until we find you, wherever you are, and both of you die. Plus those other people Hector mentioned. Tortured first, then killed. All of you."

The thought of him torturing us evidently excited him. His eyes glistened. Maralita's lips trembled.

"Anything else?" I said, trying to keep from slugging the son-of-a-bitch. I had to step away for a few seconds to calm myself.

"Yeah, a couple of other things. When you're given the money in Providence, take a count with the contact present. Let him verify the amount, then both you and the contact call in to me with the agreed-upon amount."

"Will do."

"Be especially careful when picking up the money. We've done a lot of business with the Providence mob before, but I wouldn't trust them. One time, after a pickup from Providence, our guy was driving through the southern end of Rhode Island when a car tried to run him off the road. The only reason he got away was because his car was souped-up and the other guy's wasn't. We can't prove it was the Providence gang, but you have to ask, who else could it be? Since then we've been extra cautious."

"Why don't you stop doing business with them?" I said.

"Because they sell a lot of drugs throughout New England, and we've made a lot of money from them, asshole."

Apparently, like the mailman, none of this exalted conversation kept him from his appointed task. He handed us our travel expenses in fifties and hundreds. He saw me look it over. "Look, wise guy, you got three grand there, plus the stolen credit cards. That's more than enough to get you to Rhode Island and then to New Mexico."

"Suppose we run into trouble and need more?"

"You got my cell phone number. Give me a call. And, by the way, don't even think about dipping into *our* money. We make a count at the receiving end."

"You don't have to worry."

"I know I don't." Gilberto ran a finger across his

throat and made a slitting noise.

I blanched. "Fuck you."

Gilberto snickered, gave me the finger and left.

Maralita and I slipped into our Salvation Army uniforms. I gassed up the car at the first gas station, and to paraphrase the race track announcer's words at the start of a race, Maralita and I were off and running.

~ ~ ~

Nightmares of Gilberto shooting the bound and gagged captive awakened me on nights with a jolt, my body trembling and bathed in sweat.

Time and time again I asked myself how in hell I had ever sunk into this mess. Yeah, I needed the money, needed it bad, not only to live decently but also to sooth my bruised ego, to show myself and the world that I could once again be successful, even if that success was a criminal enterprise.

I just never imagined that it would involve violence. Naïvely, I didn't associate smuggling money with murder. I thought all of the violence would be confined to smuggling drugs, not transporting drug money.

Wake up, stupid! Stealing money from Mackles' payroll office was kid stuff comparted to what you're involved with now. You've graduated to playing in the big leagues, where murders are as commonplace as rain.

I had been foolishly naïve. Illegal money attracts all sorts of tough and nasty people such as thieves, gangsters, murderers plus local cops and federal law enforcement agencies like DEA and Homeland

Security. Not exactly my league.

All of this new experience was overwhelming to me, an ordinary white-collar worker whose greatest fear until getting laid-off from Bowkart had been an approaching thunderstorm. How I yearned to reverse the clock and jump off this crazy bandwagon.

But it was too late. I needed the money, making me in for the ride. Nonetheless, I had no illusions about Hector. I got the strong impression that, like the Mafia, once you signed up with the Sinaloa cartel, you were a member for life.

"Long term" wasn't a phrase I would use regarding my anticipated tenure with the Sinaloa cartel. I was a gringo, not a Mexican, and like the Mafia, they clung to their own and discarded everybody else. If I wanted to assure a long life I would have to plot my way out of the cartel's grasp. It wasn't going to be easy, but my life and Maralita's life may depend on it. Which means I needed a stash of money for Maralita and me to disappear and live our lives comfortably and anonymously, far, far away from Hector and Gilberto and the Sinaloa cartel. Perhaps in Australia or Hong Kong. Somewhere on the other side of the globe.

Time to get a handgun, regardless of Gilberto's instructions to the contrary. And that I intended to do before Maralita and I reached the Rhode Island border.

FIFTEEN

"How far to Richmond? I said.

Maralita opened the roadmap and ran her finger along the route from Colombia, South Carolina to Richmond, Virginia. "Looks like 375 miles. I'm estimating the time to arrive there," – she paused and calculated –"about six hours, maybe a little more."I reached inside my shirt pocket and brought out my Republic Wireless smart phone and handed it to Maralita.

She looked puzzled. "So?"

"Get online and lookup a website called Armslist."

Maralita knew her way around the Internet. After a couple of minutes, "Okay, I got it."

"Armslist is a firearms marketplace where private parties and gun stores sell weapons online. Handguns, rifles, shotguns, ammo. There's an advantage to purchasing a used gun from a private party. It's normally a guy who isn't particularly interested in who he's selling to, as long as he gets his price in cash. That way I can get a gun not registered to me. That's the kind of gun we need. Something untraceable."

Maralita said, "But he will have your name."

I smiled. "No, he won't. I'll show him one of my fake licenses if need be. Hell, a lot of guys selling guns never even ask for ID. All they want is the money."

"Oh." Maralita frowned.

"What's wrong?"

"Querida, we're not going to use a gun, are we?"

"It's only for protection. Nothing else."

"But I never needed a gun before."

Meaning when she was smuggling money. "You couldn't if had you wanted to. Not on an airplane. Look, don't worry. I just feel more secure with a gun in the remote – I said remote – chance we need it."

She didn't look convinced, but nodded yes anyway.

"Now, look under the state of Virginia and read me the listings for handguns."

Maralita scrolled through the website and said "Wow. They list hundreds of guns."

"Now look up a category that says '9mm Luger."

It took Maralita about five minutes to scan the list. "I found over 200 guns alone. That's a lot. What now?"

"Okay, now read me off private party sales in the Richmond area for 9mm handguns. Private parties. Not gun stores."

"Don't you care about the price?"

"No time for that right now. Read me off the listings."

As she came across each she read it to me and I told her to send an email to owners of 9mm handguns I selected with these words: *Interested in buying your listed gun and ammo for cash, provided you can meet early tonight in Richmond. Will let you know where around 6:00 p.m. Send phone number.*

About forty minutes later, Maralita had sent out a half-dozen emails for 9mm handguns. Three of them Berettas, one Glock, one Kimber and one Kel-Tec.

"Okay, you can rest your pretty fingers now." I reached over and took her hand and kissed the fingertips. She slid over in the seat and buried her face in my neck.

"Isn't buying a gun from somebody online illegal?"

I snorted. "Not now, but if the anti-gun nuts have their way, they'll confiscate every weapon from every decent citizen in this country, leaving them defenseless and at the mercy of criminals who will have the only guns remaining."

"Guns make me nervous, querida."

"Me, too. Don't get concerned." I patted her hand.

~ ~ ~

We rolled into Richmond around 5:00 p.m. and found a low-price motel called Broadview Guesthouse and checked in, using one of our stolen credit cards. I opened my Laptop and found five responses to my ad for the 9mm handgun. Best of the bunch was a Beretta 9mm with a 13-round capacity and an extra magazine. Bingo!

I called the party selling the gun, a guy with a voice that sounded like a hasp sharpening a file. Probably a redneck wearing a NRA cap, but what did I care as long as the Beretta was in good condition. Still, to protect myself I decided to meet him at a local mall that Maralita and I had passed on our way to the Broadview Guesthouse.

I peeled off the Salvation Army uniform and replaced it with everyday civilian clothes. No sense in giving away our disguise.

About thirty minutes later I pulled into the mall

parking lot. I saw the gun seller's brand new and gleaming red Ford pickup truck where he said he would park it, close to the mall entrance. I parked my car nearby and walked over to his truck. He saw me and opened the passenger-side door and gestured for me to hop in.

I slid into the passenger seat and gave the guy a once over. He was tall, gaunt, unshaven and dressed in clothes that looked and smelled as if they hadn't been washed in a month. And he wore a John Deere cap. Redneck Supreme.

"You the guy wants the gun?" he said.

"That's me. The Beretta."

He brought the Beretta out from under the driver's seat along with a spare magazine and laid them on the seat between us. "Here she is. Had the gun six years now. Just as good today as the day I bought it new. Thirteen rounds plus one in the chamber. With the spare magazine, you got 27 rounds of pure firepower." He snickered and revealed stained yellow teeth, one of them missing.

"The gun's condition?"

"Hell, look it over," he said with resentment creeping into his voice. "I take care of my guns."

The gun did look well cared for. "How much?"

"How about 700 dollars?"

"Any ammo?"

"You got twenty-seven rounds, mister. The rest you buy yourself."

"I'll give you 500."

The redneck leaned back in his seat and squinted at me as if he were aiming down the barrel of a rifle.

Chills swept up and down my spine.

"Suppose I throw in an old Kel-Tec. A P-11, holding 10 rounds of hot 9mm firepower."

"Let's see it."

He reached over and snapped open the truck's glovebox and handed me the P-ll. The grip was worn and some of the bluing had rubbed off the barrel. Otherwise it looked okay. "Is it loaded?"

"Expect me to carry around my guns unloaded? Do I look like a dumb hick?"

He sure as hell did, but I let that slide. "I'll give you 700 cash for both."

He rubbed his chin as if deep in thought. I could hear his fingers scrape across the stubble of his unshaven face. "Okay, you got a deal."

I started to pick up the guns when he said, "Hey, not so fast. Let's see your driver's license."

I was prepared to show him one of my stolen licenses, then thought better about it. "Sorry, cash is all you get." I swung open the passenger side door as if to leave. He reached over and gripped my arm. "Hold on, mister. I'll take it."

I pulled out a wad of hundred-dollar bills and peeled off seven and handed them to him. He didn't take his eyes off the bills, nor my wad, like a hungry dog salivating over a chunk of raw meat. He dropped the guns and spare magazine into an empty Wal-Mart bag. I took the bag, got out of the truck, climbed into my Chevy Tahoe and drove back to the Broadview Guesthouse.

~ ~ ~

I got up to pee around 3:30am and noticed

somebody passing by our motel room window. In the middle of the night? It put me on edge. I took the Kel-Tec P-11 and held it behind me as I opened and stood behind the door and glanced around the parking lot. The Chevy Tahoe was parked directly in front of my room.

All of a sudden, the door flew open and knocked me backward into the room. The P-11 flew out of my hands and landed under the window drapes.

It was the redneck. He was pointing a handgun at me. He reached behind him and shut the door. "Get up, city boy."

Maralita jumped up from the bed and gasped. Her eyes were wide with fright. It distracted the redneck long enough for me to scramble across the floor and get my hand on the P-11 and turn to face him.

But it was too late. He placed the muzzle of his gun on my forehead and I froze. I wasn't sure I could bluff him, and I was afraid he might shoot me. I dropped the P-11 to the carpet.

"Let me have the rest of those hundreds you were flashing."

Maralita snarled "pendejo," at the redneck and he thrust his gun in her direction. The distraction was all I needed. The redneck pivoted his gun back toward me, but I got to him first. From the floor, I grasped the barrel of the P-11 and swung the butt of the gun up as fast and as hard as possible, and it smashed into his balls. The breath whooshed out of him and he uttered a squeaky noise and dropped to his knees and bent over. He was gathering breath to shriek but he didn't have time because I hammered the back of his head with the butt of the gun. He collapsed silently, his handgun skittering across the floor. A thin stream of blood from his head trickled down the back of his neck.

I sat where I was on the floor and the shakes started. Maralita leapt from the bed to the floor and rushed to me on the floor.

"Are you okay, querida?

"Don't worry about me. Look out the window," I said. "See if we attracted attention."

She rose and opened the door and scanned the parking lot and motel. "Nothing. It's quiet."

She came back into the room and sat down on the edge of the bed. Both of us were silent for a few minutes. My pulse gradually stopped racing and the shakes vanished. I picked up the redneck's gun, a Glock 9mm, from the floor and threw it in my suitcase. From no guns to three guns in one night, all 9mm, which makes it easier when buying ammunition.

Maralita glanced at the redneck. "Is he alive?"

I felt the carotid artery in his neck. "Got a strong pulse."

"Who is he?"

"The guy I bought the guns from. He must have followed me back here and waited till it was quiet enough to rob us."

"What do we do now, querida?"

"We dump him."

"But won't he identify us to the police?"

I smirked. "I doubt the cops would believe anything he claims. The guy's a bum, a redneck.

Besides, he doesn't know who we are."

"But the motel knows. We checked in wearing our Salvation Army uniforms."

"Don't worry about it. I paid with cash and signed in with phony names. At cheap motels like this, they don't check closely. We'll have left Virginia before anybody knows we're gone."

I looked at the time on my cell phone. "Just about 4:00 a.m. We got to get him out of here before daylight. Let's get moving."

We slipped into our Salvation Army uniforms and packed our bags. While Maralita loaded the Tahoe, I found the redneck's truck keys in his pants' pocket. I also found the seven-hundred bucks I paid for the guns, and pocketed it.

Now that I had three guns, I thought it might be a good idea to load one in the secret compartment that would contain the money, the 750 grand. Making sure that nobody was looking, I opened the trunk and lifted the floor mat and punched in a code number in the electronic device that sprung open the concealed compartment. I set the Kel-Tec P-11 handgun inside and closed the compartment and replaced the mat. The Glock belonging to the redneck went into the glove box of the Tahoe and the Beretta beneath the driver's seat.

"We'll load him in his truck and I'll drive it and park somewhere far enough away from here. You'll follow me, then we'll come back and check out of the motel and get back on the road."

I found the redneck's pickup truck and parked it next to the Tahoe. It was still dark outside and nobody in sight. The redneck wasn't all that difficult to carry and place onto the passenger's seat. He was skin and bones, about 150 pounds. His rank smell made the task difficult. Maralita wrinkled her nose.

I hopped into the driver's seat and started the truck. The redneck was slumped over in his seat, his head resting on the window. It appeared as if he was sleeping.

Maralita followed me in the Tahoe. About five miles down the road I found what appeared to be a deserted store. I drove around the back and parked the truck with Maralita close behind me. The redneck stirred and I clobbered him on the jaw three times with my fist until he passed out again.

Maralita drove us back to our motel. We checked out and hit the highway. Neither of us wanted breakfast. The redneck's rancid stench still clogged our nostrils.

~ ~ ~

I'm a TV cop show aficionado: *Cops, Law and Order, Jail, Homicide, Las Vegas Jail, The Wire, The Shield.* You name the cop show, I watch it. So I understand some of the more common rules of law used in arrests. By clobbering the redneck, I had graduated from simple theft at Mackles to theft and felonious assault, both serious felonies.

What troubled me most was that it didn't bother me in the slightest. I really wanted to beat the shit out of the redneck for attempting to rob me, and I did. *Goddammit, it felt good. I was sick of getting the short end of the stick and I wasn't in the mood to take anybody's shit. Not anymore.*

The same for the money. It didn't concern me one iota that I now obtained my income through criminal acts. I was only concerned with not getting caught and hauled off to jail, then to prison.

I'm not the same Sam O'Hara I had been for the first 50 years of my life. The old Sam O'Hara hadn't been in a fight since grade school, and avoided one at all costs. Nor had he abused other people.

I couldn't blame the change entirely on my dire economic circumstances. Lots of people lose their jobs and don't go around robbing and beating up people.

It had to be how my father had ingrained in me the notion that society measures the worth of a person, not based on his good acts, but how successful he is. And, let's face it, most successful people in business don't really give a rat's ass how ruthless they have to be to achieve success. The important thing to them is not how they arrive at the pinnacle of their profession, but the simple fact that they *do* get there, whatever it takes.

Say hello to the new Sam O'Hara.

SIXTEEN

In Marine Corp boot camp I once explained to a couple of farm boy recruits from Nebraska how business was conducted in my home state, Rhode Island. "When I was ten-years-old I wanted a bike. Mom and Pop could have bought one at Ann & Hope, a large department store at the time, but it was cheaper to buy one from some guy Pop knew. The guy said he could supply one that 'fell of the truck' at about half the cost of an Ann & Hope bike.

"That was how we bought stuff we needed. Stolen goods. Saved my family a pile of money. A washing machine, furniture, whatever. All of it dropped off the back of a truck."

Thing is the Providence Mob controlled Rhode Island and everybody and everything in it. Including the law. We never got caught with stolen property because the cops and their families also took advantage of buying stolen goods at reduced prices. Besides, most cops were bought off by the Mob. Not a pile of money, except for the top cops of course, but enough to make them turn in the other direction when the Mob conducts its business.

In fact, the whole damned state is crooked, from politicians to businessmen to everyday people like my family. It's a way of life.

Give you another example. Drive from say Connecticut into Rhode Island and the first thing you notice crossing the state line, the roads turn bad. Pot holes, cracks, uneven surfaces. Rhode Island roads are unfit to drive on. The worst in the country. That's because tax money slated for roadwork improvement goes into the greedy politician's pockets, not to mention the pockets of crooked road contractors.

Like it or not, this is the way we did things in Rhode Island. Believe me, nobody in their right mind, I mean *nobody,* challenged the Providence mob.

~ ~ ~

This was the first time I had returned to Rhode Island since my mother's death, shortly before I joined the Marine Corps and departed for Parris Island, South Carolina and boot camp.

It was early summer and the weather was mild. But I paid scant attention as my mind was focused on the Providence mob. These guys were notoriously lethal. Cross them, fail to fulfill your part of a deal or just glance at them sideways and you were liable to find your throat cut and your body dropped into a hole in the woods of Arcadia Management Area in western Rhode Island, a park with 14,000 acres and a lot of buried secrets.

If the Providence mob met with your fancy, you were likely to come face to face with guys whose first names and nicknames were something like Jimmy Bagels, Baby Fat Giuseppe, Mush Face Pat and Tony Cheeks. Those names might make you chuckle but you would be kidding yourself if you thought they were a barrel of laughs.

Besides the usual racketeering income sources such as drugs, whores, gambling, extortion, money laundering and human trafficking, the Providence mob had a lucrative sideline: contract killing. Need somebody to disappear? A bothersome neighbor making a play on your wife? An adversary for a promotion at work? An abandoned girlfriend trying to get even? These guys can accommodate you and will for a negotiated price.

The Providence mob had so much clout in Rhode Island they probably could have advertised in the newspapers and on TV and gotten away with it. Like I said before, nobody was foolish enough to challenge them.

According to the grapevine, the boss of the Providence mob had FBI connections. Not unusual, since Whitey Bolger, boss of the Winter Hill gang in Boston, served as an informant for the FBI. And the FBI, in turn, allowed Whitey to remain in power for many years.

To clear my mind, I drove Maralita around Rhode Island to show her the beaches, Newport, the gilded age mansions, the church where Kennedy and Jackie were married. Tourist stuff. She loved every minute of it. It took her mind off our assigned task, which was to walk into the lion's den, collect $750,000 and walk out with our skins intact.

The tour lasted a few pleasant hours. Now it was time to get to work.

~ ~ ~

When I lived in Rhode Island, Federal Hill was 100 percent Italian-American. If you weren't Italian-American you lived elsewhere. Nowadays it has a mixed population, still mostly Italian-American, but with blacks, Hispanics, Native Americans and Asians added to the mix. Lately, there has been some talk of resettling Somali immigrants on Federal Hill. Not that the original inhabitants like the changing demographics, but that's the way it is.

To rub salt in the wound, Federal Hill had become a tourist attraction. Since the advent of *The* Sopranos on TV, and Scorsese's Goodfellas and *The Departed* in movies and on DVDs, tour busses and curious travelers rode and walked the streets peering into shop windows and trampling the lawns of private homes looking for gangsters. It made no difference that the gangster flicks were based in New Jersey and Boston. Prying tourists needed their Mob fix and they came to Federal Hill to get it.

All of this was enough to drive out some members of the Providence mob. They relocated their homes to the towns of Cranston and Warwick, to name a couple. And that's where Maralita and I headed. We used the Tahoe's GPS to direct us to the one specific address Gilberto provided, a private home in Warwick, close to the Providence airport. The home of Bruco Cancellera, the capo di capi tutti, or in popular terms the Godfather, of the Providence mob.

I found Bruco's address and parked adjacent to the curb in front of his home. It was a small two-story wood-frame house, freshly painted, with a small well-tended front lawn. Lace curtains decorated the windows. A detached garage completed the picture. Nothing out of the ordinary. It was similar in size and construction to homes in the surrounding neighborhood. Homes, for the most part, owned by such citizens as department store employees, barbers, grocery store owners, cops and firefighters.

My first reaction was how come the top dog in the Providence mob doesn't live in a twenty-room mansion on 10 acres surrounded by a steel fence. Sort of like Hector. My second reaction was more sensible. Because it would draw attention to him, and given his occupation, the last thing he wanted was to spit in the eye of the public and the cops by displaying his ill-gotten wealth. Hey, look at me. I'm king of the hill and I live like royalty, way over the head of you common folks.

By contrast, Hector lives in luxurious surroundings, but that is Mexico, and this is the United States. One hell of a difference. There, he is king of the Sinaloa cartel, and one of Mexico's most powerful and prominent citizens. Few have the courage and connections needed to challenge him. And few do. Not those who enjoy living. So he lives like he wants to live.

Living downscale for Bruco Cancellera made a lot more sense and brought a lot fewer headaches. Mobsters in the USA do not have anywhere near the power of the federal government. If they get too big for their britches, Uncle Sam will crush them. Keeping a low profile pays off.

As I remember, even the cars Providence mobsters drove were Chevys, Fords, Buicks, Chryslers. Nothing fancy and nothing foreign.

Neither was Bruco's car. It was a Buick, maybe six or seven years old, and it was parked in front of a detached garage alongside his house. A Chrysler 300 and a Ford pickup truck were parked behind the Buick.

Maralita and I straightened our uniforms, donned our caps and exited the Tahoe. We walked up to the front door of the house and rang the doorbell.

A face quickly parted the lace curtains. Moments later the front door opened. An older woman around sixty or so greeted us with a cheery smile. Most of her hair was missing, and that which remained was wispy.

She said, "We contribute to the Catholic Church, but I'm sure we can spare the Salvation Army a few dollars."

She noticed us glancing at her head. "Oh, it's all right. I have the cancer and lost my hair after radiation. I used to have a full head of chestnut hair." Her eyes shone in remembrance.

Her New England accent was thick. She pronounced cancer as cahnser, heavily accented on the first syllable. People in New England don't drive the car to market. They drive the cah to mahket. It took me 10 years to shake that accent after I left Rhode Island.

She smiled again. "It doesn't really bother me, you know," she said referring to the cancer.

I had known cancer survivors before. People who were grateful to be alive, especially those who found Jesus after their ordeal. They lighted the room with their presence. This woman was no exception.

"We're not here seeking a donation, ma'am," I said. We're here to see Bruco."

"Oh, you mean Daddy. Why didn't you say so? Please come in." She opened the door wide and

Maralita and I stepped inside.

"Sorry to hear about your troubles, ma'am," Maralita said.

The woman touched Maralita's arm. "I'm doing just fine, thank you."

The dim entrance hallway was decorated like a shrine with crosses centered around a large picture of Jesus on one wall. The other wall exhibited family photos, some of them I guessed dating back 50 years.

"Daddy has trouble talking nowadays. But my brothers Frank and Joseph are there to help."

She escorted us to a small parlor where all three men were sitting around the TV, watching a soap opera. The old man, presumably Bruco Cancellera, boss of the Providence mob, sat in a motorized wheelchair. He looked half dead. His rheumy eyes glanced at Maralita and me without expression.

The woman said, "These nice people are here to see Daddy." She pointed at one of the men and said to us: "This here is Frank and the other is Joseph, my brothers." She smiled and left the room, closing the door behind her.

Both of the men, Frank and Joseph, stared at us as if we were creatures from outer space who had unexpectedly materialized in their home.

"What can we do for you?" Frank asked. He was lean and grizzled with penetrating eyes that seemed to measure my every move. He was dressed in jeans and an undershirt, displaying arms of sinewy muscle.

"We're here for the money," I said. "Gilberto sent us."

"You're not Salvation Army?"

"No, we're not."

Frank snickered and turned to Joseph, who was a carbon copy of Frank, just a few years younger. "Looks like Gilberto got the Salvation Army doing his work for him."

Joseph had a dead eye with scars surrounding it. One of those scars, fiery red, ran from his eye to his ear. He looked us over with his one good eye and returned his gaze to the TV. I painted scary pictures in my mind, imagining how Joseph got those scars.

"We were told to contact Bruco," I said.

Frank pointed at his father. "He's in no condition to talk. I'll do it for him."

"We're here to pick up the money," I said.

Frank examined Maralita from head to toe. "Never seen a nice-looking woman in that outfit before. Ones I seen are fat and dumpy."

Joseph looked her over with his one good eye and grunted, then turned his attention back to the TV.

"Does she talk?" Frank asked.

"Only when she wants to. And she doesn't want to right now."

Maralita threw an elbow in my side as a warning.

"What she wants," I said more forcefully, "is to count the money."

A smile broke out across Frank's face and he slapped his knee. "Goddamn, boy's got some fight in him," he said to Joseph.

Maralita jumped in. "You don't want to cross Hector."

The smile froze on Frank's face. Her words stopped Joseph who was just about to say something, probably something nasty. Evidently, even members of the Providence mob were fearful of Hector's clout.

"Look," I said, "we're here to pick up and count the money. Not to cause trouble. That's the arrangement."

Frank nodded to Joseph. He hopped out of his chair and moments later I heard cars being driven away from the garage.

"We've got your money in a locked safe underneath the floor in the garage," Frank said. "We can count it there. Backup your car to the garage. Cutie and I will meet you there." He winked at Maralita. She looked frightened but I nodded to her and she went with him.

Joseph had already moved the Buick, Chrysler and Ford truck out of the driveway and onto the street. I backed the Tahoe up the driveway until the trunk was almost hitting the garage door. Joseph opened up the garage and Frank, Maralita and I entered. Joseph closed the garage door.

"Turn around," Frank said, "and face the door. When we open our safe, we don't take a chance that nobody can see the combination. I'll tell you when we're ready."

Maralita and I did as we were told. While we faced the garage door I heard electronic tumblers clicking and an electric motor humming.

When Frank told us to turn around I saw a heavy steel gate on the floor swing open and a large metal pallet rise from a cavity underneath the floor. The pallet contained stack after stack of neatly bundled and packaged bills piled high and held together with long, thick rubber bands. It was reminiscent of that scene from the TV series *Breaking Bad,* where the character that Brian Cranston plays has collected so much money from cooking and selling meth, that he can no longer launder money, and has to pile bills on a wooden pallet in a rented storage space.

In one tiny corner of the metal pallet, nine orderly stacks of banded money, each several inches high, were held together with wrapping paper and the name Gilberto written on it with a black marker. Frank pointed at those stacks and said, "That's your money."

"Pretty clever way to hide cash," I said.

"Damn tootin'" Frank said. "We paid a ton of money to get the damn thing installed, but let me tell you, ain't no son-of-a-bitch going to rob us."

Maralita looked at our stacks of cash. She was skeptical. "It doesn't look like 750,000 dollars."

Frank said, "Don't talk to me, talk to Joseph. He's our accountant in charge of the count."

Joseph peered at me with his good eye. "The stacks, are each about five inches high. They contain both fifties and hundreds. There are approximately 1165 bills per stack. Assuming an even split between the denominations, each stack is worth about $87,375. Total amount for all nine stacks combined should be $786,375, give or take a few dollars."

My mouth fell open. This from the guy who looked like he just got back from the bad end of a knife fight. The same guy who a few minutes ago was being entertained by a TV soap opera. Wonders never cease.

"Joseph knows his numbers," Frank said, with brotherly pride in his voice. "We don't need another count."

I shook my head. "Maralita and I been instructed to make a count, get the exact dollar amount in each stack and you or your brother verify our count."

Frank had a nasty expression on his face. "That's a pile of useless work."

"It's the way Hector told us to do it," Maralita said.

The magic name, again: Hector. Frank slapped his hands alongside his thighs in frustration. A slew of foul-mouthed invective flew out of his mouth. "Then let's get it over with."

We moved the money to a workbench in the back of the garage. Maralita and I opened the first stack and started counting. When we made our count for that stack, Maralita wrote the tally in a pocket-sized notebook she carried in her purse, then turned the stack over to Joseph who checked our count.

"This is going to take some time," Joseph said. "We're talking over 10,000 bills."

It took us about three hours. By the time we finished, Frank was ready to fly off the handle. Not a patient guy like his younger brother.

Maralita and I tallied the count. "Our total is 785,900, close to your estimate, but $250 short of your count."

"Jesus, who gives a shit?" Frank said, and threw his hands up in the air.

I ignored Frank and called Gilberto on my Republic Wireless smart phone as instructed. "We're

$250 short of their count."

"Then you eat the $250, wise guy," Gilberto said.

I felt the blood rush to my head. "I've had enough of your bullshit. Just let me do my fucking job and you hand over the 50 grand you owe Maralita and me when we deliver the money."

Dead silence over the phone. "You giving me an 'or else', pendejo?"

"Count on it." I hung up the phone. Frank was grinning at me while Joseph said, "Let's load your car."

Frank opened the garage door. I managed to stop shaking long enough to pop the trunk and slide open the secret compartment. Maralita and I loaded the money, and I closed and locked the compartment and shut the trunk.

We drove off as Frank and Joseph stood at the garage door sneering at us, or more probably, me.

After we had been in the car for about fifteen minutes, I pulled into a McDonald's parking lot. Both Maralita and I breathed a long sigh of relief. We had entered the lion's den and emerged without a scratch.

We got back on the road. Destination Las Cruces, New Mexico.

SEVENTEEN

Since my abrupt departure from Bowkart Industries and my torturous and unsuccessful search for meaningful employment, I had coarsened, and I knew it. I'd become belligerent, suspicious and ready to inflict physical pain at the first sign of resistance to my needs.

That wasn't me. Not the real me. At least it wasn't in my previous life. Stealing payroll dollars wasn't the real me. Half-killing rednecks wasn't the real me. Smuggling drug money wasn't the real me.

Except it was.

Before getting unceremoniously dumped from Bowkart, like just so much flotsam, I never gave any thought to the predicament of unemployed people. Sure, I watched sad stories about homeless people on TV, read online and in newspapers and magazines about the ever-increasing rate of people without work, heard horror stories of families thrown out of their homes, but none of this personally touched me or affected my everyday life. I was self-absorbed, battling the memories of a daughter who tragically died young, a first wife who left me bereft, a second wife who used me and stole everything I owned, and loss of most of the equity in my home by conditions beyond my control.

Life on the unemployment line hardens you, but it also makes you more sensitive to the plights of other unfortunate people. I now felt the hardships and struggles of unemployed people because I was among them. I found that without meaningful work, providers – both men and woman – find it difficult to hold their heads high. It was no longer incomprehensible for me to stand in their shoes and feel their pain.

Depending on food stamps to put food on the table shrinks their souls. Being unable to find new jobs destroys their self-confidence. Losing their homes and the sweat-equity that went into their purchase obliterates their sense of self-worth.

Resorting to crime changed everything for me, some aspects for the better, some aspects for the worse. On the upside, it pays better than working a white-collar job. The anxieties of wondering where the next dollar is coming from were gone.

On the downside, I was dealing with some of the meanest, greediest and scariest people imaginable, much worse than the corporate cutthroats of my previous existence. I had to stay constantly on guard for violent confrontations. I was learning to expect and anticipate challenges at every juncture from every criminal I encountered along my path. Yes, it was possible that I would be caught and sent away to prison. Or that my life could suddenly and brutally end, without mercy.

But I chose this path and I intended to make it work for me. If you look at the odds, my chances of steady work were much better as a criminal than as a white-collar worker. Simply, that is what I wanted all along: a job with a future.

~ ~ ~

We were driving on Interstate 78 just east of Harrisburg when I noticed the radiator was overheating. I pulled over to the right-hand lane and left the Interstate at the next exit.

I drove into the first spot that looked like a garage, not just a place to gas up and buy a sandwich and soda. Maralita and I got out of the car.

A mechanic dressed in greasy overalls stood in front of the garage and eyeballed our Salvation Army uniforms without a glimmer of interest. One of his cheeks was engorged by something that was either gum or chewing tobacco.

While Maralita stretched her legs, I told the mechanic about the overheating problem. He popped the hood and checked the radiator with a flashlight. "I don't see the leak," he said. "Let's put the car on the hydraulic lift and take a look from below."

It wasn't gum he was chewing, it was tobacco. He spit a huge wad of juice that must have flown 10 feet before it landed on the cement driveway in front of the garage.

I wrinkled my nose in disgust and drove the Tahoe into an inside stall. He directed me with hand signals until the car was positioned on the hydraulic lift. I shut down the engine and got out.

He raised the car on the lift and checked the radiator from underneath.

"Found it," he said. "Looks like a small piece of metal punctured the radiator, just enough to cause a leak. Kind of crap you pick up on the highway when people discard their soda cans without waiting to find a garbage container." He shook his head in dismay at the don't-give-a-damn drivers who litter the road. "I can fix it in a jiffy."

I thanked him, and got a couple of Diet Cokes from the soda machine and brought one to Maralita.

"If you have to use the bathroom," I said, "do it here. We're already behind schedule, and our lord and master Gilberto, might dock us some of our pay if we arrive late in Las Cruces."

As she left to find the restroom, the mechanic came up to me and tapped my shoulder. "Come over to the car. I want to show you something funny."

My heart jumped into my throat. *Holy shit, he's found the money compartment.*

We walked over to the lift, and he pointed to what appeared to me a hunk of metal stuck to the inside of the wheel well on the passenger's side.

"What's that?"

"It's a real-time GPS tracker in a weatherproof magnetic case."

"A tracker?"

"It's a GPS just like in new cars. It shows you where you are on the map. But this one goes a step further. It tracks you as you're driving."

"You mean somebody can tell where we are at all times?"

"That's exactly what it means. Somebody put that GPS in your wheel well. It didn't get there by itself." He spit out another wad of tobacco juice that flew out of the garage. This wad flew farther than the first wad. I wanted to congratulate him on setting a new record.

He reached in and yanked the device from the wheel well. "This powerful magnet holds it," he said, as he wiped his mouth. Let me suggest that you buy a GPS jammer. That way if anybody attaches a GPS to your car, the jammer will block the signal."

But I wasn't thinking about GPS trackers or GPS jammers. *Thank God he didn't find the hidden money compartment.*

I pocketed the GPS device and waited while the mechanic soldered the leak in the radiator. When he finished, I thanked him profusely and tipped him 50 bucks over and above the bill for uncovering the GPS tracker. Maralita and I climbed into the Tahoe and left.

"We've got to stop somewhere again," I said. "We need to talk, and I want to show you something."

Maralita looked annoyed. "I thought we were in a hurry."

"We are, but this is more important."

She looked at me with a puzzled expression.

"Patience, my dear. Patience."

~ ~ ~

Just west of Harrisburg, we drove into a Denny's and parked.

We found a seat in the restaurant near a window where we could keep an eye on the Tahoe. The waitress, an older woman with a sour expression, took our order and brought us coffee while we waited for our lunch. When she was out of hearing range, I told Maralita about the GPS and removed it from my pocket and placed it on the table. It sat there like a hand grenade between us.

"Somebody's tracking us?" Her eyes flashed alarm. "Who is it?"

"My first thought was Bruco's sons, Frank and Joseph. But we're a long way from Providence. From what I remember about them, the Providence mob pretty much confines their shenanigans to New England."

"Then who could it be?" Maralita asked.

"There's only one other person I know of. That's Gilberto."

Maralita said, "Maybe he's just tracking our mileage to make sure we keep to the plan."

"I don't think so. My second thought was that if Gilberto believes we might take the money and run, the GPS tracker will allow him to find us. My next thought was maybe Gilberto plans to hijack the load for himself and kill us, then tell Hector we ran off with the money."

Maralita reached across the booth and squeezed my hand. "Maybe that's what we should do, querida. Take the money and run."

That comment stopped me cold. I stared at her. "You've got to be kidding. That's the fastest way to get Hector on our ass. And I don't believe we *ever* want Hector on our ass. That's the kiss of death. You're not serious about taking the 780 grand, are you?"

Maralita shrugged. "It's just a thought."

Every now and then Maralita both surprised and frightened me. Reaching for the gold is one thing. Placing our necks on Hector's chopping block is sheer suicide.

In corporate America we have a phrase called risk aversion. It means that a manager will choose the lowest risk path when confronted with choices.

Maralita was the exact opposite. Appalling risks did not seem to deter her. She proved that by smuggling money into Mexico and serving time when she was caught, without revealing Gilberto or Hector's involvement.

She proved it again when she persuaded me to transport drug money across the country.

And now she was proving it once again by wanting to steal the entire pot. Hector's pot.

I put the kibosh on the idea. I stomped it to death. I explained to Maralita in no uncertain terms how foolish it was.

Maralita reluctantly agreed. But I sensed this wasn't the last time I would hear from her about the 780 grand.

When we left Denny's, I searched the parking lot for an out-of-state license plate and found one on a new Cadillac with Nevada plates. When nobody was looking, I bent over and stuck the GPS inside the car's passenger-side wheel well.

I chuckled. *If it was Gilberto who planted the GPS tracker, he'll pitch a fit when he discovers it isn't attached to the Tahoe.*

EIGHTEEN

We decided to call it a night when we reached Roanoke, Virginia. Including the time lost to repair the radiator, we had been on the road about 15 hours and we were worn out. The experience with Frank and Joseph, the Keystone Kops of the Providence mob, was enough to frazzle anybody's nerves. Finding a GPS tracker on the car topped it all. Enough for one day.

We checked into a cheesy inn called SlumberRest along Interstate 81. It was just what you'd expect, a place to spend the night one level above a hot sheets motel.

Not that we cared. Maralita and I showered, then collapsed on the bed, too tired for sex, too tired for dinner. In moments we fell asleep, Maralita in my arms.

A sudden noise startled me and pulled me from a deep sleep. I jumped to a sitting position and reached for my Beretta. Maralita was still out cold. I frantically looked around the room and saw nothing out of the ordinary. Then I noticed my smart phone. It was vibrating and jingling. I reached over Maralita to the night table and grabbed the phone and walked to the bathroom and closed the door. I didn't want to awaken Maralita.

"Yes," I said, my voice thick with sleep.

"Where the fuck are you?" It was my charming friend Gilberto.

If Gilberto had placed the GPS tracker on the

159

Tahoe, then why was he now asking for our location? I cleared my throat. "We're in Roanoke, Virginia, on the way to Las Cruces."

"What motel?

I told him.

"Wait a minute." There was a silence on the phone for a couple of minutes, then: "I just looked at a map. I want you to make another stop before you deliver the goods."

"Another stop? For what?"

"For a pickup, asshole."

"Don't pile on me, Gilberto. I'm not in the mood. Just tell me what you want."

Another silence. I could hear him breathing hard.

"You need to go to Memphis. According to *MapQuest,* it's about a 10-hour trip from Roanoke. You'll make the pickup at this address." He read me the address and I repeated it, searched for a pencil and paper, found them and wrote it down.

"I need a name."

"It's a woman. Her name is Jennifer Stevens, the Reverend Jennifer Stevens."

I guffawed. "You've got to be kidding. A minister?"

"This minister you're making fun of is one of our best accumulators. So just shut the fuck up."

"I wasn't making fun of her."

"You know, asshole, as soon as this trip is over, you and I are going to have a 'come to Jesus' meeting."

Gilberto was a stone killer. He wouldn't hesitate to kill me or anybody else who interfered with his business. A shudder rippled through me. But the last thing I wanted was for Gilberto to think he had me cowed. I steeled my voice and said, "How much?"

"How much what?"

"The pickup. How much?"

A momentary silence again. "One point one."

Jesus! One million, one-hundred-thousand dollars. I peeked outside the bathroom. Maralita was sleeping soundly.

"Okay, we'll get underway in the morning."

"Like hell you will. Get started now."

"Fuck you, Gilberto, it's 1:30am. We'll start in the morning." I hung up.

~ ~ ~

After eating breakfast at a nearby MacDonald's, we found our way onto Interstate 40 and drove west toward Knoxville, Tennessee.

"What's a collector, Maralita? Gilberto said our next stop is to pick up money from this lady minister who's a collector."

"That's one of our mules who gathers payments from drug dealers and distributors so Hector's people – that's us in this case – can make one pickup instead of five or six. It's a smart move. The fewer the number of pickups the less our exposure to the cops and the DEA. Hector uses accumulators everywhere the Sinaloa cartel does business."

"How about the Providence mob?"

"I'm not sure, but I guess they act as their own collector since they sell drugs throughout New England."

I drove in silence for several hours as Maralita took a long nap. When she awakened, Maralita turned on the radio and found a Spanish-speaking station.

The blare of a mambo assaulted my ears.

"Great idea. That music is keeping me awake." I smiled at Maralita and she reached over and gently pinched my right arm and smiled back.

About two hours later I spotted a tail.

"Turn around in your seat slowly, look behind us," I told Maralita. "See that black Dodge Charger?"

She peered out the back window. "I see a black car."

"What state is the license plate?"

"I think it's Pennsylvania." She bent over the front seat and peered out the back window to get a closer look. "Yes, it's Pennsylvania."

"We don't know anybody in Pennsylvania regarding our work, do we?"

"No, I don't know anybody there."

"Does Gilberto?"

Maralita shook her head no. "Not that I know of. He never mentioned anybody he knows in Pennsylvania."

It was quiet for a while as Maralita and I examined our memories for possible memory lapses. We didn't find any.

Maralita said, "How do you know he's following us?"

"When we checked out from the motel this morning I saw the car pass by. Didn't pay any attention then, but I saw the same car in the diner's parking lot. That same car is behind us now. It may be a coincidence, except I no longer believe in coincidences." I looked over at her. "Gilberto knows where we spent the night."

We locked eyes for a moment. "Do you think –"

"It's got to be Gilberto tailing us."

In my previous existence as a white-collar worker, I had been fat, dumb and happy and unaware of surrounding dangers. Now I was acutely aware of everything going on around me, and everybody I came in contact with. The life of a criminal sharpens your senses, brings your fear to the forefront. And fear is a prerequisite for survival.

Fear ignited Maralita's eyes. "Who is it, querida?"

"Damned if I know. I'm still unsure if that car is following us. Let's find out."

At the next exit, we left Interstate 40 and drove south on Route 66 toward Pigeon Forge. The black Dodge Charger followed us. I checked to make sure my Beretta automatic was handy and I told Maralita to get the Glock out of the glove box. The Kel-Tec P-11 was in the secret money compartment.

Between the two loaded and available handguns we had 23 rounds of 9mm hollow point ammo, ready and waiting plus a spare magazine of 13 rounds. I chambered a round into the Beretta and showed Maralita how to do the same with her P-11. She struggled with it, but managed to load a round. I prayed to myself that we wouldn't get involved in a firefight, but swore to shoot off very round to defend myself and Maralita.

"How many persons in the car?" I asked Maralita. "Did you notice?"

Maralita had broken out in a sweat. Her hands shook, and I wasn't sure she would be able to help me when the shit hit the fan.

"Two. I saw two."

"That's the way it looks to me. Let's see if we can flush them out."

I spotted a diner down the road and pulled into its parking lot. A large flashing neon sign alerted us to the fact that we had arrived at Carl's Diner. I counted twenty-one cars and three large articulated trucks, which meant the diner would be busy with hungry patrons. That's helpful. Thugs – I assumed the men in the Dodge Charger were thugs – would not cause a scene in front of that many witnesses.

I slipped the Beretta inside my waistband and told Maralita to tuck the P-11 in her purse.

We entered the diner and found a booth facing the parking lot. Diners stared at our flashy Salvation Army uniforms. Within a minute or so, the Dodge Charger rolled into the parking lot, but too far away to see the occupants clearly.

"Let's order some food, Maralita." I said.

"I couldn't eat right now if I had to."

"At least get a milkshake. Something to nourish you."

We both looked out at the parking lot where the Dodge had parked. So far, nobody had exited the vehicle.

"Get you something, honey?" the waitress said. She was short with a disproportionately huge bust, what we used to call bazoombas in high school. Funny how even in the most dire circumstances a guy will notice that.

"Give her a milkshake and I'll have a tuna sandwich and a diet Coke."

"Coming up, honey."

Maralita stared at me and frowned. "Pay attention to the Dodge, querida. Nothing else."

"Sorry, you're right. But it does lessen the stress of the moment."

Maralita frowned. "Not for me, it doesn't."

The waitress served our lunch and we ate while keeping watch over the black Dodge Charger and its occupants.

"What's next?" Maralita said anxiously.

"Got an idea. Watch me."

I opened my cell phone and dialed 911. The 911 operator promptly answered. "911. What's your emergency?"

"My wife and I are sitting in Carl's Diner on Route 66, south of Interstate 40. We've been threatened by two men driving a black Dodge Charger. They accosted my wife and slapped her when she wouldn't give them sex."

"Are you both okay? Is your wife seriously injured?"

"I don't think so. We managed to escape inside the diner. Please help us. We're elderly and scared to death."

The 911 operator's voice was tense. "Police are on their way."

"I think they have guns," I said, knowing that the mention of guns will send out a whole bunch of cops, all armed to the teeth, to make a "guns drawn arrest."

I hung up and called the waitress over and paid the bill and left her a nice tip.

"Do they have guns?" Maralita said.

"I'd bet on it. If they're following us, and it looks as if they are, they'll have guns."

"They're after the money, aren't they?"

"Let's go," I said to Maralita, ignoring her question, the answer which was apparent as a rising sun at dawn. "Just do what I say."

We both entered the vestibule of the diner and watched the Dodge Charger through the door window. Within five minutes the parking lot was swarming with police. They surrounded the Dodge Charger, weapons drawn, and yelled, "Hands up! Get out of the car and get on the ground!"

"Now," I said. "Let's go." I held my arm around Maralita and guided her to our Tahoe. We got in, and in the commotion that followed, eased our way onto Route 66 north. As we passed the Dodge Charger we saw two men face down on the ground, officers leaning on their necks, crushing their heads into the asphalt while other officers cuffed them.

At the Interstate 40 intersection we followed the signs to Interstate 40 west.

What's next? What else could possibly happen?

NINETEEN

We drove until we arrived in a Memphis suburb and spent the night at a dump called Sun Vista Motel. Over breakfast the next morning, I opened my laptop and checked the Knoxville News Sentinel, for arrests. A small article appeared:

The Knoxville Police Department arrested two men in the parking lot of Carl's Diner yesterday afternoon as the result of a 911 call regarding a possible assault and attempted rape.

According to the 911 operator an elderly man claimed that two men in a Dodge Charger slapped his wife when she refused to have sex with them.

When the police arrived, the elderly couple had left the diner. The two possible assailants were identified by the car they were driving, a black Dodge Charger. When the police confronted them, they tried to escape but were blocked by police cars.

Both men were carrying handguns without licenses. They were arrested for that charge as well as resisting arrest. They were booked at the county jail, pending arraignment.

According to the police, both men, Dominic Petiago and Rudy Gambrini have arrest records dating back 10 years and have been associated with the Bombanno crime family of Philadelphia.

I slid the laptop across the table so Maralita could read the story.

Here eyebrows furrowed. "I don't know either of those two or the Bombanno crime family. Never heard of them. What do they want from us?"

I snorted. "The money, what else? Somebody told them we were carrying 780 grand and they decided to heist it. For the life of me I just can't figure who that somebody is."

"It can't be Gilberto," Maralita said, as she closed the laptop and returned it to me.

"You're right. It doesn't make sense that he would steal the money from himself, unless −" I stopped and snapped my fingers. "Unless he's trying to steal the whole 780 grand *for* himself, minus what he pays those two gang members from Philadelphia for robbing us."

A shadow of fear passed over Maralita's eyes.

"Maralita, I know what you're thinking. Because Gilberto knows how ruthless Hector is, he's the least likely person to double cross him."

"I'm not worried about Gilberto. I'm worried about us. If it's true that Gilberto's behind this and he succeeds in taking the money, we'll pay with our lives as well as Gilberto. Hector will think we were involved."

"You're right, and the best way to avoid trouble is to pretend those two gangsters in the Dodge never happened, make the next pickup in Memphis, then deliver the money as agreed to Las Cruces, New Mexico. As soon as we do we call Hector, tell him about Gilberto and the two Philadelphia thugs, and let him know the money was delivered as promised."

Maralita nodded. "That's probably the best bet."

I winked at her. "Stick with me, kid, and you'll see me sprout lots of ideas, most of them worthless."

We had a good stress-relieving laugh over my comment. Once the laughter subsided, I said, "But look, we've falling behind schedule. Let's get back on the road. We've got an appointment with a lady named Jennifer Stevens in a couple of hours."

~ ~ ~

The address Gilberto provided was just outside the eastern perimeter of Memphis, on the edge of open country. The Tahoe didn't have a GPS so Maralita played navigator with a roadmap. She guided me when we left Interstate 40 and headed south.

The church, if you want to call it a church, was a sprawling single-story ranch. It had the appearance of the owner starting with a small two-bedroom ranch and adding different sections to it over the years. A large neon cross mounted on the roof and dominating the far section of the ranch appeared to be hovering over the home's largest space. This, apparently, was the church where the congregation worshiped.

An equally large sign composed of fading black plastic letters near the road announced the home of *The Church of Our Heavenly Mercy*, a church I had never heard of, until I reminded myself about the proliferation of denominational churches across the South.

The house was rundown and in need of a fresh coat of paint, and the church's front lawn was filled with weeds. The overall effect was tacky, and maybe this impression was deliberate. It would be the perfect cover for somebody working in the drug business.

Nobody in his or her right mind would associate a thriving criminal enterprise with this shabby church and home.

I parked the car in the gravel parking lot and Maralita and I got out and entered the church through the front double doors. It was cool and dark and quiet inside. We had to stop for a few moments to adapt our eyes to the low light.

The church was empty, but as I stood in the vestibule and looked upon the alter and the statue of Christ, memories flooded back. Pleasant memories of the Catholic church where my mother and father and I worshipped. Better, more innocent days.

I was reluctant to leave, but Maralita squeezed my hand and I abruptly stopped daydreaming. We left the church and walked around to the front door of the home and rang the doorbell.

"Is this the rectory?" Maralita whispered.

"I don't know if they call it that," I whispered back.

The front door swung open and a portly lady with swept back snow-white hair stood in front of us and smiled. "I'm Jennifer Stevens," she said and offered her hand. "You're really not with the Salvation Army, are you?"

"We were sent by Gilberto."

She awarded us with a warm smile. "Well then you must be Sam and Maralita. I expected you yesterday."

We shook hands all around, and I said, "Sorry about the delay. We had some unforeseen problems."

"No matter," she said, "please come in." She

ushered us into a welcoming and comfy living room, that was the opposite of the home's dilapidated exterior. A fireplace with a large stone mantle took up one wall. Comfortable butter leather chairs and a matching leather sofa surrounded an ornate lacquered coffee table with inlaid tiles. A walnut bar cart service on wheels stood nearby. Paintings of Tennessee mountains and valleys adorned the walls. It was a rustic setting, but one in which I wanted to kick off my shoes, plop down in a soft chair, drink a cup of coffee with brandy thrown in and enjoy relaxed conversation with this nice lady.

How can a minister afford expensive furniture and furnishings on her salary from the church? I answered my own question: *Because she's handling drug money, stupid. And there's a ton of money to be made for one and all.* As Gilberto said, this woman was a major money collector in the Sinaloa cartel and one of its more successful associates.

The portrayal of Jennifer Stevens and her house and church was deceptive. When I met her, I thought of one word that captured her essence. That word is congenial. She had a smile that radiated happiness, although the wrinkles around her eyes hinted at sorrow.

Furthermore, she was an ordained minister. None of this you would expect from somebody associated with drug smugglers and money launderers. It made no sense. Jennifer Stevens was a puzzle, a paradox.

"Reverend Stevens, we have to take a count of the money and report the number to Gilberto before we leave. Maralita and I will need you to verify the dollar amount."

"Naturally. That's standard procedure. Before we

get down to business, may I offer you some lunch? And please, call me Jennifer."

Maralita and I accepted. The three of us ate a fresh and delicious fruit salad and lounged around the dining room table drinking coffee afterward.

"Jennifer," I said, "I know it's none of my business, but I'm going to ask you, anyway: How in the world did you get caught up in the drug business?"

Jennifer's eyes clouded over. "My husband has dementia. He's living in a nursing home, a very expensive one. The Church's health insurance policy is very limited. I had no choice. The money Hector pays me makes it possible."

"Oh, sorry to hear about your husband," Maralita said, and I added my condolences.

"This was his church and this was our lives. We were both ordained ministers. This has been our home for thirty-two years." She swept her arms out as if to embrace her home and her past. "Once he became" – her voice choked – "once he became too sick to work, I assumed his responsibilities." She turned away, choking back tears.

After Jennifer regained her composure, I told her about the incident with the Dodge Charger and asked her if she had ever heard of the Bombanno crime family in Philadelphia.

She tapped her cheek and thought about it. "You know, in this business you hear all kinds of rumors, some of them reliable, most of them not. And you do meet a lot of unsavory people, present company excepted, of course. You both seem vastly more civilized than the people I normally deal with in the

172

drug trade. But, yes one of my associates in Little Rock, Arkansas mentioned a connection between Gilberto and the Bombanno family. I have no idea what that connection is, but he claimed it was business oriented. Which means drugs."

Maralita and I exchanged glances. Jennifer picked up on it. "Look, I don't know you two well, but you look honest. At least as honest as one can expect in this ugly business. No insult intended." She paused to collect her thoughts. "The older couple before you, I don't remember their names, but the last time they were here for a pick up, they received a phone call. I don't know what that call was about, but the next thing I know somebody I didn't recognize drives up to the church in a Chevy van and honks the horn. The older couple got in the guy's van and off they go without a word to me when they intend to return. Never saw them again. Gilberto called me and instructed me to hold onto the money until he could send somebody else to pick it up. That's been two months now."

I said, "How large was that shipment?"

"One point one million dollars. That's what you're here to pick up and deliver. I don't mind telling you I've been a nervous wreck holding it. The disappearance of the older couple scared me."

Once more, Maralita and I exchanged glances. I saw the fear in her eyes and I imagine she was thinking what I was thinking. *What happened to the older couple?*

Jennifer rose from the table and motioned us to follow her. She guided us through the house to a garage attached to the back. Two cars were parked side by side, one of them a new Chevrolet Impala, the other an older Subaru Forester SUV.

"The Chevrolet Impala is mine," Jennifer said. "The Subaru belongs to the older couple. It's been parked here since they left unexpectedly. When they didn't come back I wasn't sure what to do with it. I called Gilberto and he said the older couple wanted out of the business and that I should keep the car or sell it, whichever I prefer. Quite honestly, I found that reply strange. You would think the couple would come back to claim it."

Maralita's lips trembled slightly. "Makes you wonder, doesn't it?"

I added, "Yes, it does."

"Well, enough of that," Jennifer said. "We still have business to transact." She led us to another small room, the size of a kitchen pantry, and slid aside a large painting on the wall to reveal a sizeable wall safe. She turned the tumblers and opened it. The safe was deep and wide. "Here's the money," she said.

We removed the bundled stacks of money and carried them into the kitchen and counted the bills. It was denominated in fifties and hundreds, standard procedure insisted on by Hector for all his customers. This time the count was exact. I called Gilberto and let him know.

"Maralita and I are staring out tomorrow morning for Las Cruces with both packages," I told Gilberto.

"That's no longer necessary. Take the 50 grand I owe you and Maralita from the package you have. I'm sending somebody else to pick up the package and deliver it. You and Maralita can leave as soon as you hand it over to him."

"But –"

He hung up on me.

With a shaky voice, I told Maralita about Gilberto's instructions. Her face turned a pasty white.

"Are we going to disappear like the old couple that preceded Maralita and me? I now understood the future Gilberto had in store for us. And it wasn't pleasant. *Had we already outlived our usefulness?* The thought sent shivers through me.

TWENTY

"There's no getting around it," I said. "Gilberto killed the older couple. Why, I don't know. For whatever reason, we've outlived our usefulness to him, and now he's coming for us. The only questions remaining are when and how."

Maralita hugged herself. The chill had nothing to do with the weather, a warm summer's day. Maralita feared for her life and so did I.

"We won't get in a stranger's car like that older couple, will we, querida?"

"We'll be long gone before this guy arrives. I'm guessing he'll be an accomplished assassin, somebody Gilberto relies on to solve his people problems. And we're now the people problem."

"How much time do you think we have?"

"I don't know, but probably no later than tomorrow morning." I looked at my watch. "It's 1:00 p.m. We better get on the road within the next hour."

"We'll take the Tahoe?"

I thought about that for a moment. "Just long enough to find and buy a used car. And, while I'm thinking of it, let's get rid of these Salvation Army uniforms. People remember us. In plain clothes, nobody will give us a second look.

"How much of Hector's money do we take?"

"Fifty –" I was about to say 50,000 dollars, our fee for transporting the money from Providence to here and on to Las Cruces. "We'll need more than fifty grand. We'll take 100,000 for our time and trouble."

"They'll come for us if we take more than the fee Gilberto agreed to."

"You're right, but fifty grand won't cut it. Not if we're going to start a new life somewhere."

"I'll tell you what we can do, querida, if we really want a new beginning. We take *all* of the money. The hundred thousand will get us only so far and then we'll be facing the same problem: What do we do next?"

"Look, one-hundred grand is peanuts to Hector. Chances are he won't bother with us for that amount. But if we take all of the almost two-million, he'll track us down, sure as hell."

"I disagree. Hector's greedy enough to come after us regardless of how much we take over fifty thousand. May as well go for the entire package. How much money do we have?"

"We have $780,000 from the Providence mob and $1,100,000 from Jennifer. Bringing the total to $1,880,000."

Maralita rushed into my arms. "It's our one chance, querida, our only chance. With almost two-million dollars we can escape and live well for the rest of our lives. Can't you see that?" Her eyes, aflame with excitement, searched mine.

"Hector will find us," I said, stubbornly, while trying unsuccessfully to avoid gazing into her eyes. "Where in the world can we go where Hector's long arm doesn't reach?"

"I know a place, querida. A place Hector will never

think to find us. A place where the sun shines very day, where the cost of living is cheap and where two-million dollars will last us a hundred lifetimes."

I couldn't help but smile. "And just where is that magic land?"

"Belize."

~ ~ ~

We shed the Salvation Army uniforms and changed into casual summer wear. Of course, I didn't tell Jennifer of our possible intention to keep the money, afraid she might call Gilberto to protect herself. Neither did I want her involved if and when the shit hit the fan. Any knowledge she had of us taking the money would make her an accomplice and a target for Gilberto.

"I recommend you get rid of the Subaru Forester SUV, the older couple's car. That links you to them, and who knows where they are. My guess is they're both dead."

Gooseflesh suddenly appeared on Jennifer's arms and she shivered. "Good suggestion. I'll get rid of it tomorrow."

"You'll have to dump it in another county, far from here. You can't sell the car because the buyer will be another link."

"Yes, I see what you mean."

Maralita and I loaded the Tahoe and said our goodbyes. I drove into Memphis until I found a used car lot and haggled with the salesman for a seven-year old Honda Accord and settled on a price. I used one of our fake credit cards to buy the car. I figured we had at least a couple of weeks before the car lot owner discovered the credit card was phony, and by then we would be long gone and the car abandoned.

Maralita and I drove off, me driving the Tahoe and Maralita in the Honda following me. I found a crowded parking lot in front of a busy mall and pulled in and parked in the back of the lot, as far away as possible from the mall entrance. It was turning dark outside, which would help keep mall shoppers from remembering our faces.

When we were sure nobody was near us, we transferred the money, all 1,888 million of it to the trunk of the Honda. We removed our bags and guns from the Tahoe, and I took the Salvation Army uniforms and tore them up with my Gerber folding pocket knife, and stuffed them in a nearby dumpster beneath a pile of garbage.

I drove the Tahoe to a nearby five-story parking lot and parked the car in the back on the second floor. When nobody was in sight I spent about thirty minutes wiping down the car with a soft rag both inside and out, to get rid of our fingerprints. I knew the Tahoe couldn't be traced to us because Gilberto had bought it, or more likely, arranged for it to be bought. Using my pocket knife, I shredded the credit card used to buy the Honda.

I'm becoming so accustomed to crime I can steal two-million dollars from my employer and purchase a car illegally without either care or remorse. Don't know whether to congratulate myself or kick myself in the ass.

Maralita waited for me in the Honda outside the parking garage and we drove off.

~ ~ ~

We stopped at a local hibachi grill for an early dinner.

"Where to now, querida?"

I shrugged my shoulders. "Frankly, I haven't stopped long enough to think about it. I'll tell you where it won't be: Las Cruces, New Mexico."

"I have an idea."

I glanced at her and chuckled. "I'm almost afraid to ask."

She reached across the table and teasingly slapped my hand. "Do you want to hear it?"

"Sure do."

"Okay, we first have to rule out returning the money to Hector."

I exhaled, showing my pique. "I'm not sure about that. What's your idea?"

"Play along with me. If we disappear with the money, Hector will blame Gilberto. He'll assume Gilberto hijacked the money and killed us."

"Maybe Hector won't assume we're dead."

"Querida, if he can't find us and the money, it's the only conclusion he can draw. He's going to want Gilberto's blood. Gilberto will take the fall and you and I will be in the clear."

If that's true, then Hector will not kill Freddie, my first wife Margaret and the others. That's a relief. The possibility of their deaths weighed heavily on my shoulders.

"If we do this, querida, we can't just put the money into a bank or investment account at a brokerage house."

I nodded. "I get that. The banks and investment

brokers notify the IRS and DEA of any large sums of cash deposited."

"Exactly. That option is out. We could put the money in a couple of large safe deposit boxes, but too many trips in and out of a bank or credit union may arouse suspicion."

"I agree. Assuming we take the two million––and we haven't decided that yet – whatever steps we take have to be done quietly and without attracting attention. Especially Hector's. Now, tell me more about your idea."

"There's an importer in Atlanta who will send our money to a location we select. A wire transfer of money on our behalf to a company in a foreign country, and list it as payment for goods we intend to import."

"What kind of goods?"

"We're not going to import anything. Let me give you an example. I mentioned Belize to you while we were in Jennifer's church. We'll talk more about that later. For now, let's say you're a furniture manufacturer and you need mahogany wood, which is hard to come by, which Belize grows in abundance. The importer in Atlanta will make out a purchase order under the name of our company and email it to a mahogany grower in Belize. It will be accompanied by a wire transfer of whatever amount of money we want to send to the mahogany grower's bank."

"Is this guy, the importer, trustworthy?"

"One-hundred percent. He's been in business twenty-five years and never once have police crossed his path."

I rested my chin on folded hands, my elbows on the table, and kept my eyes focused on Maralita. "This is beginning to sound workable."

"It gets better. The mahogany grower will deposit our money in his bank under his company's name, and the bank will hold the money until we show up in Belize and either withdraw all of our money from that bank or keep it deposited there and conduct our banking there. In any case, that money remains ours. For this the importer, the mahogany grower and Belize bank will charge us about five percent each."

I whistled. "Wow, that's fifteen percent of our money, almost 300,000 dollars."

"We'll still have a million and a half. More than we need to live a life of luxury."

"Is the mahogany grower real?"

"Yes he is, but like everyone else, he likes to make extra money on the side, so he owns his bank and takes deals like ours."

I whistled. "Cute, really cute. I'm just amazed at you, Maralita. You really know the ins and outs of handling illegal money."

Maralita's raised her eyebrows. "That displeases you?" She attached no "querida" to that statement.

"I didn't say that. Hell, I'm lucky I have you by my side, and I know it."

Maralita's features softened. "Tu eres el amor de mi vida, querida." You are the love of my life, darling.

"I love you, too, Maralita, you know that. Now, how did you learn about this importing company?"

"Before connecting with Gilberto and Hector's organization I worked for them."

"I find it hard to believe the owner of that importing business would tell you about his illegal sideline. It could get him in trouble with the law."

Maralita grinned like a little girl caught stealing cookies from mama's cookie jar. "He didn't tell me, querida. Doris, the lady he works with who makes the arrangements with foreign companies confided in me."

"I've said it before, and I'll say it again, Maralita. You never fail to amaze me."

Maralita blew me a kiss from across the table.

"Now tell me about Belize. You mentioned it when we were with Jennifer."

A noisy party of six diners sat down next to us. Maralita said, "Let's get in the car, first, away from prying eyes and ears."

I paid the bill and we left the restaurant and climbed into the Honda in the restaurant's parking lot.

Her eyes were focused far away in a distant time as she reminisced. "When I was working as a flight attendant, we flew to Belize every week. I loved the country, even more than my native Mexico."

"What do you love best about Belize?"

"Perhaps the absence of the type of violence we see in Mexico, where the Federales and cartel sicarios kill each other by the thousands." Her face turned grim. "There's so much unnecessary death. I never feel safe in my home country anymore."

"What else do you love about Belize?"

"The people are easy to get along with. There are many cultures, and they seem to blend together. It's the only English-speaking country in Central America. The second most popular language is Spanish. We would fit in well, querida."

"Any native tongue?"

Maralita nodded. "Kriol, a mixture of English, Creole and who knows what else thrown in. But everybody speaks English."

"When you say the natives are easy to get along with, you mean they are laid back? Not uptight and tense like Americans?"

Maralita folded her fist and pretended she was going to slug me. "They're all just as easygoing and sweet as you, querida."

We both enjoyed a hearty laugh. It eased the tension we both felt about stealing Hector's money.

"Well," Maralita said. "Are we going to do it?"

I looked at her sitting beside me in the car and out eyes met. "Yes, we're going to do it."

We kissed, and in that moment our fate was sealed.

"It's going to take a lot of planning," I said, "and the guts to actually get it done."

"I believe in us, querida. We can and will do it. Successfully."

"Okay," I said, and took a deep breath. "Let's get going."

Maralita opened the glove box and took out a roadmap and plotted our way to Atlanta, Georgia. "It's going to take us about six hours."

I glanced at my watch. It was 6:30 p.m. "We'll drive there now, rest up in the morning at your apartment, and be at the importers once it opens.

No Jobs Available

When Gilberto finds out we disappeared with Hector's money, the shit hits the fan. This will give us a jump on him."

We found our way onto Interstate 22 and drove south.

TWENTY-ONE

The offices of Ahmed Erkan were located in an old office building in a decaying section of Decatur, Georgia, a suburb of Atlanta. Maralita and I rode the creaky elevator to the fifth floor. Erkan's office was the first past the elevator. The chipped sign on the frosted glass door told us that we had arrived at *Erkan's Global Importing, Inc.*

We knocked on the door and walked in. A broad-shouldered woman with dyed red hair and a lit cigarette dangling from the corner of her mouth was seated at a desktop computer typing furiously. Her nimble fingers danced across the keyboard in a blur of motion. When she saw us, she stopped abruptly.

She removed the cigarette from her mouth and said, "Yes?"

"Don't you remember me, Doris?" Maralita said.

Doris looked puzzled for a moment, then her face blossomed into a smile. "Hell yes, I do." She rose from her seat and embraced Maralita. "Haven't seen you in a dog's age, honey." Her voice floated between baritone and bass.

"This is my boyfriend, Sam O'Hara."

The lady gave my hand a bone crushing handshake. "Nice to meet you, Sam."

"Me too," I said as I winced and nursed my sore hand.

Maralita said, "We have an appointment with Ahmed."

"Then, by God," Doris said in a thundering voice,

"I'll show you right in cause he's in there by his lonesome."

As Doris ushered Maralita and me into Ahmed Erkan's office, Maralita whispered in my ear, "Doris is a male."

"No shit," I whispered back. "I couldn't tell."

Ahmed Erkan was a small, wiry man with a thick mustache that made him look like Buffalo Bill. He hugged Maralita and shook my hand.

"You're a lucky man," he said to me with a distinct Middle-Eastern accent.

I grinned. "Don't I know it."

"Please," he said, waving us to two chairs in front of his crowded desk, piled high with papers, empty coffee cups and an assortment of pencils and pens.

We sat down, and I said, "Thanks for taking our call yesterday. As we both mentioned we are interested in your –"

Ahmed held up us hand to stop me from saying any more. "Please. I know exactly what you're interested in. You need mahogany for your furniture plant. Understandable. It's hard to come by. How much are you interested in buying, in terms of dollars?"

"My manufacturing budget will allow for $1,880,000."

"Yes, yes, a good amount. I can work up an estimate of how much mahogany that buys. And, of course, you can confer with the grower to determine how much you need at exact times in your manufacturing schedule and in what form and quantity."

Not mentioning specifically what we were really interested in – moving our money overseas in a format that doesn't arouse the suspicion of the IRS – was a smart operating philosophy. You never know who's listening in, especially in this cyber age where the CIA, FBI, NSA, DNI, Homeland Security and who knows who else is tapping into our lives, listening in and watching our every move every day.

"You are interested in purchasing the mahogany from Belize, yes?"

"I am. I understand they have a lot of it for sale, and the quality is high."

"It once was Belize's number one export. It no longer is, but the country still produces and exports a high grade of mahogany."

"That's what I want for my furniture factory."

Ahmed said, "You, of course, have the money, yes?"

"It's in–"

I was going to say "cash" until he interrupted me again. "Yes, I understand what you mean. Perhaps you and Maralita could take some time now with Doris to make arrangements? When you are done, I'll provide the name of the grower and his contact information."

I started to rise. He stopped me again as I was half-way up from my seat. "The fee for my end will be five percent, and of course the grower and his bank will each have its own fee requirements. There may be a small additional fee for converting American dollars to Belize dollars."

He shrugged his shoulders when my eyebrows raised at the words 'small additional fee.' "Belize

No Jobs Available

governmental requirements. You understand the government must always take its share. Is this satisfactory?"

I said yes and Maralita and I left Ahmed and met Doris in her office. She winked and suggested we go outside to get some fresh air.

"Where's the money?"

"In our car." I pointed to the Honda.

"Drive it around to garage number six."

I got in the Honda and followed the driveway around the back of the office building where several small garages, the size of large sheds, perched side by side. I drove into garage number six. Doris and Maralita met us inside and locked the garage door. We unloaded the cash and spent the better part of three hours making the count on the hood of the Honda.

"Done," Doris said, "$1,880,000. Our fee will be five percent." She removed a small electronic calculator and tapped the keyboard several times. "That's $94,000. The remaining balance is $1786,000. Agreed?"

Maralita and I agreed.

"I'll take it from here." Doris called Ahmed on her cell phone and verified the amount for the "purchase of mahogany wood from Belize."

"Is that it?" I said, when we were done.

"That's it," Doris said. "Ahmed will give you a receipt and the money will be wire transferred either this afternoon or tomorrow morning at the latest to your new contact in Belize. Either Ahmed or I will call you when the wire transfer has been completed."

Maralita tugged on my sleeve. "Let's go."

~ ~ ~

We drove to Atlanta and spent the night at the Ritz-Carlton in Buckhead, treated ourselves to dinner at Bones, one of the best steak restaurants in the Southeast and finished the night at Johnny's Hideaway, a cross between a nightclub and a pickup joint, on Roswell Road. We fell into bed at the Ritz-Carlton about 2:30 a.m. half-drunk and giggling.

At 9:30 a.m. my cell phone rang.

"Is this Sam O'Hara?"

I was groggy but managed to croak out that I was.

"This is Ahmed Erkan. The transfer is complete. I am texting you the grower's name, email address, phone number and office address in Belize, as well as a receipt for the commission you paid me."

I thanked Ahmed. He gave me instructions for contacting the grower in Belize, wished us good luck and hung up.

With our business now complete and our money safely transferred to Belize, Maralita and I could breathe a sigh of relief. I Called Delta and booked a flight for both of us the following morning from Atlanta to Belize City, Belize using our fake identities and a phony credit card.

Maralita and I spent the day shopping for new clothes at Lenox Square and Phipps Plaza, both high-end malls in Buckhead. We crashed early that night at the Ritz-Carlton, exhausted from our cross-country trip.

The following morning we hitched a ride with a Ritz-Carlton bus to Hartsfield-Jackson International Airport. After checking in using our fake passports for identification, we waited at the gate for our flight. I bought an *Atlanta Journal–Constitution* newspaper from a magazine vendor and handed Maralita part of the paper.

As I was reading the business section Maralita gripped my arm and exclaimed "Mierda."

Startled, I turned to face her. She handed me a folded-over section of the newspaper and pointed to an article. I took the newspaper and read it.

An early evening attempted robbery in Decatur led to the deaths of two business people who were closing up their office for the day.

Ahmed Erkan, owner of Erkan's Global Importing, Inc., was gunned down in his office and killed. His assistant, Doris Whitaker was also shot and killed, apparently by the same assailant.

Police say there was evidence the assailant thought the office was empty and made a lot of noise in an unsuccessful attempt to open the safe. A witness in a nearby office heard the racket and saw the two victims rush to the Erkan's Global Marketing office from the public restroom on the fifth floor. Several gunshots followed. The assailant ran from the building, and the witness called the police.

The police do not know the assailant's name and the witness did not get a good look at the assailant in the dark hallway to make a positive identification. His identity remains a mystery.

I lowered the newspaper and stared at Maralita. She was gulping air as if there was a short supply.

"This is too much a coincidence," I said.

"Hector. It has to be Hector."

"My guess is Gilberto. He sent those Philadelphia goons after us to steal the money, the two thugs from the Bombanno family."

"But, querida, Gilberto knows nothing about where we are."

My brain raced into overdrive. I snapped my fingers. "The phony credit card at the Ritz-Carlton. He may have traced it. But how did he know about Ahmed Erkhan?"

Maralita gasped. "I just remembered something. When he hired me to smuggle money into Mexico, I told him I had worked for Ahmed."

I nodded in ascent. "Had to be. Gilberto found out we weren't in the Tahoe heading for Las Cruces and was probably racing around furiously, trying to find out where we are. Even assuming he knew about your former connection to Ahmed, how could he possibly know we used Ahmed to transfer money to Belize? Doesn't hang together."

Maralita and I gazed at each other in silence. Finally I said, "If he's the killer, could be he found some paperwork about us and Belize in Ahmed's office."

"Never. Ahmed and Doris were always careful not to leave a paper trace. It would have exposed their business. My guess, querida, this has nothing to do with us. Most likely, it was a thief who knew there was a safe in Ahmed's office."

We both stopped again and stared out the window of the terminal as if the answer to our predicament resided in the planes arriving and departing from the airport.

"Well, we're going to find out," I said. "We have no other alternative but to go to Belize. That's where our money is."

TWENTY-TWO

A s soon as we disembarked from the Delta flight in Belize City and cleared customs, I saw a man holding a handwritten sign on a large piece of cardboard: *Erkan's Global Marketing.*

"Are you looking for me?" I asked him.

The man had shoulders so broad and hands so large I'd bet he could hug and uproot a six-foot-diameter, one-hundred-foot-high mahogany tree all by himself. He looked Spanish but had the prominent cheekbones and flat nose and impenetrable eyes of a Native American. Maralita said he was a Mestizo, a mix of Central American and Native American.

But he sure as hell didn't look like any chauffeur or cab driver. Alarm bells started ringing in my head.

He spoke only Kriol with a little Spanish thrown in. Maralita interpreted for me. "Are you Mr. O'Hara, the American that was in Mr. Erkan's office two days ago?"

I said I was.

"Show me your receipt from Mr. Erkan."

"Whoa, not so fast," I said to Maralita. "Who is this guy and who does he represent?"

She asked the man in machine-gun-rapid Spanish. "He says his name is Pasqual and he represents Señor Mateo, the farmer and mahogany grower. He sent him to pick us up and take us to the señor's business."

I recognized the name. Ahmed Erkan gave it to me, specifying Mateo as my contact in Belize.

"Where is Señor Mateo's business located?"

Pasqual with the dead eyes said, and Maralita interpreted, "In Rancho Dolores, about 30 miles from here."

I opened a map of Belize I had taken from the Delta flight and looked up Rancho Dolores. "That's in the countryside," I told Maralita. "I ran a quick online check on Belize last night. From what I saw the farther you get from the cities, the more dangerous it becomes. I don't like it."

Maralita looked irate. It had been a long and tiring trip from the time we picked up the Tahoe in South Carolina until here and how. Enough danger and anxiety to frazzle anybody's nerves. "Querida, Señor Mateo is the person holding our money. Ahmed said that's where we have to go to get it."

"You don't seem to be particularly concerned."

"I'm not. I trust Ahmed."

I grunted. Something deep inside me was sending out SOS signals to my brain. I wrote if off to nerves. Like Maralita, I had been on edge since Gilberto gave us our marching orders for the money pickups. Each subsequent adventure on our journey in Richmond, Knoxville, Memphis and Atlanta had done nothing to calm me. Especially since the murders of Ahmed and Doris.

I sighed. "Okay, here's the receipt." I handed it to Pasqual who held it close to his face and examined it like a first-grader learning to read, his brow furrowed. He handed it back to me and said "Okay." Dumb as he appeared, the guy was cagey enough to put on a convincing act. I doubted he could read English.

Pasqual led us out of the airport, pushing through throngs of excited travelers, Maralita and me in tow. He escorted us to his car, a four-wheel-drive Isuzu Trooper. I got in the front with Pasqual and Maralita climbed into the back.

If you've ever visited Belize you're familiar with the small buildings crowded together, a hodgepodge of streets and alleyways, the smell of different foods in the air, a heady mix of Creoles, Mayans, Mestizos, Americans, Europeans and a dozen other nationalities, all commingling in relative harmony. What you won't find is Starbucks, high-rises, large department stores or chain groceries. Visitors accustomed to the lifestyles and accommodations of Western culture are invariably anxious to return home.

It didn't take any time before we left paved roads and bounced along on rutted dirt roads barely wide enough to contain the Isuzu. Branches from palm trees slapped the sides of the car loud and often enough to startle Maralita. She shifted from her position near the door to the center seat.

We passed the Spanish Creek Wildlife Sanctuary and entered Rancho Dolores. Besides an occasional church and a few shacks by the roadside the only other signs of life were farms and cattle. Farther on we came across several large sheet-metal buildings with tractors and other agricultural equipment parked in adjacent lots.

Pasqual drove onto the parking lot of a small

wood-framed building with a sign in the single window facing the road. The sign read *Mateo Industria Agroalimentaria.*

"We get out here," Pasqual said in halting English. I raised my eyebrows and exchanged glances with Maralita. We didn't know Pasqual spoke any language other than Spanish. As we entered the building I whispered, "Be careful" to her.

Pasqual led us through a shop stacked with harrows, plows, cultivators and machinery such as drill presses, grinders and shears. This helped ease my anxiety. The business appeared legitimate. I relaxed somewhat, although not enough to let my guard down.

Pasqual pointed to the back of the shop. "Señor Mateo is in the back office," he said.

We entered an office in the rear of the building, but there was no Señor Mateo. I was shocked to find Gilberto perched on the edge of a desk with a shit-eating grin plastered across his slimy face.

And even more shocked to watch Maralita rush into his arms.

Pasqual closed the office door and kept his back to it. He folded his arms across his chest and watched us.

I suddenly felt weak in the knees. "Maralita ..." I choked but couldn't continue.

Gilberto snickered. "You fell for it, gringo. My woman and I fooled you."

I staggered back until my back was against a wall.

"Maralita and I figured it right. You're an out-of-work, out-of-luck, white pendejo ready to be sucker punched. And we sucker punched you."

Maralita clung to Gilberto, her eyes shut, and said nothing.

Gilberto sneered, "You brought the money to us. All of it. Maralita and I will enjoy spending every last centavo, and remember the dumb expression on your face as we're spending it."

Maralita kept focused on Gilberto. She spoke in a chilly tone of voice I had never heard from her before. "To be exact $1,786,000. We had to pay Ahmed his fee."

Gilberto smiled. "Too bad Ahmed couldn't live long enough to enjoy it. Or the others."

My head shot up. "What others?"

Gilberto disentangled from Maralita and walked across the room and got in my face. "How about the lady in Memphis, Jennifer Stevens?"

I gasped. "Jennifer Stevens is dead?"

"The poor lady was shot in the head," Gilberto said, in a voice mimicking a crybaby.

I was stunned at Gilberto's viciousness, his casual disregard for human life. *Shit, I shouldn't have expected anything else.*

"That's not all. Remember those two Philadelphia gang members chasing you, Dominic Petiago and Rudy Gambrini from the Bombanno family? They were supposed to kill you and take the money, but you outsmarted them. Got the cops to handle it for you. You're not all dumb, are you pendejo? Well, those two are no longer a problem." He raised a hand and made believe it was a handgun, and blew imaginary smoke from the end of the barrel.

I said nothing, too shocked to talk. I stole a look at

Maralita but she was focused on Gilberto. The fondness in her eyes shattered me. *How could I have been so stupid? How could I have missed the signs? Steering me to Ahmed and then on to Belize. Persuading me to steal almost two-million dollars from Hector. The Bombanno thugs knowing where to find us.*

"To close the trail we had to kill Ahmed and Doris." Gilberto shrugged. "Too bad. They came in handy at times. But there will be others. There always are."

"Then it's been you and Maralita right from the start?"

"She was wasting away in Atlanta. I came and saved her, and once you entered the picture, I knew you were the lamb we needed to lead to slaughter. An out-of-work white collar worker with no prospects."

"Hector will figure it out," I said.

"Not a chance. Know why?"

"He'll blame me."

Gilberto guffawed. "Give a cigar to El Stupido." He laughed uproariously. When he calmed down he said, "But we are going to save him the trouble of finding and killing you. You are going to die and both you and the money are going to disappear. The money will go with Maralita and me. Hector will believe you stole the money and abandoned Maralita. You will be killed and taken up in a small airplane and dumped in the ocean with chains wrapped around you so you never surface. Nobody will ever find you. No matter how hard Hector looks."

My heart was thumping wildly. I felt dizzy. My

knees buckled and I leaned back against the wall again to keep from falling down.

Gilberto raised his hand and Pasqual walked up to me. He removed a barber's straight razor from his pants pocket and opened the blade. Its razor edge gleamed from the sunlight hitting it through the venetian blind slats of the window.

I was having trouble breathing. I broke out in a cold sweat.

Gilberto walked up to Maralita and turned her away. "You don't want to see this." She stole one last look at me and I saw in those fleeting moments a spark of compassion in her eyes. *She still feels something for me, if only sympathy.*

Pasqual got behind me, then unexpectedly and swiftly slipped behind Gilberto, reached around and lifted Gilberto's chin with one powerful hand and slit his throat with the razor in the other hand.

Gilberto flopped to the floor, his eyes wild, his hands futilely trying to stem the flow of blood from his neck. His body shuddered, the heels of his boots tapping the floor in a dance of death.

"Gilberto!" Maralita screamed and stood over him, paralyzed.

Pasqual opened the office door leading to outside the building and two burly men entered. He signaled to them and they came up on either side of me and grabbed and held my arms.

Pasqual jerked Maralita to him. She screamed as he spun her around and yanked her hair back and slit her throat.

I passed out.

TWENTY-THREE

When I regained consciousness, the two thugs who had held my arms while Pasqual killed Maralita were lifting me from the Isuzu Trooper and shoving me into the cabin of a small two jet-engine plane. I managed to peer over their shoulders and noticed that we were on a paved airstrip carved from the jungle.

Pasqual and the two thugs piled in behind me and shut the cabin door. We squeezed into tight seats, the thugs behind and in front of me. Pasqual, evidently the boss of this delightful group, signaled the pilot and we were shortly airborne and flying over the jungle.

I was still groggy but managed to ask, "Where are we going?"

One of the thugs, who was the mirror image of a caveman, answered in broken English. "You got choice. We drop you in water or in jungle."

Apparently, the two thugs thought this was funny. They both roared with laughter.

The other thug, who looked mean enough to eat live puppies, added these words in better English, "We'll wrap you in chains when we drop you from plane to make your trip down faster."

That comment broke them up, and they bent over, howling with laughter, tears in their eyes.

"Basta," Pasqual commanded in a sharp tone. Enough. The two thugs immediately brought their laughing spell to a screeching halt. They sat back in their seats and peered out the airplane's windows.

I was in a daze but my mind was on Maralita. *Oh, Maralita, why, why? Why did you turn on me? I believed it when you said you loved me.*

I forced myself to stop feeling sorry for myself. I didn't know my fate, but I vowed not to show Pasqual and his thugs how devastated I was. It wasn't much to hold onto, but it was something and it kept me from going bananas.

About three hours later we landed on another paved airstrip in the jungle and taxied to the hanger at the end of the runway. I wasn't sure where we were. Could have been Mexico, Guatemala, Honduras, maybe Nicaragua. Nobody mentioned our destination.

A black limousine with tinted windows greeted us. The thugs escorted me off the plane and dropped me in the back seat of the limo and sat on either side of me. Pasqual sat opposite us and kept his eyes on me.

We left the airstrip and climbed on twisting roads through hills. I wasn't sure of our location, but I noticed lots of palm trees, ferns, cactus and a variety of thick vegetation.

Unlike Belize, with its mild climate, this place was hot. It was summer and about ninety-five degrees outside. The limo's air conditioner was on full blast, and still the air was stuffy.

Where in God's name are they bringing me, and for what? And why? It couldn't be good, but at least I was still alive and unharmed, and for that I was grateful. I silently prayed for help and good luck. As I was beginning to realize, good luck is preferable because of the two, it's the one most likely to happen.

As we drove around another curve in the road, the limo driver turned into and stopped before a large gate attached to a high steel mesh fence. Then it came to me. Hector! This is Hector's estate.

My heart accelerated faster than an Indy 500 race car driver burning rubber from the starting line, and I had a sinking feeling that the end of my life was hours away. *That's why they brought me here. Hector wants personally to see me die. Maybe kill me himself.*

The limo driver punched a code into the entry kiosk and the gate swung open and we rode up the hill to Hector's spectacular mansion.

Except this time it didn't look spectacular. In my panicked state it looked like a mortuary. A mortuary that was about to claim my body.

The same two goons I saw my last time here stood watch, one holding an Ak-47, the other a M-16 grenade launcher. Both looked just as vicious now as they did then. Some things never change. Or was that impression the result of my fevered imagination?

This time a welcoming Hector didn't greet me at the front door. Instead, the two thugs hauled me around the back of the house and onto a staircase that led to the basement. At the bottom of the steps, they pushed me through the maintenance area and unlocked the steel door I remembered with revulsion from my last visit here. It opened into the room where I had watched Gilberto shoot one of Hector's errant employees in the back of his head. Chills coursed through my body and I dreaded what I knew was sure to follow. *This is it. Dear Lord, take me in your embrace.*

The two thugs pushed me into the same seat the errant employee had sat in when he was shot in the back of his head. They pulled my arms and hands behind my back and tied them to the chair. Then left the room and locked the steel door behind them.

I must have sat in that room for the better part of an hour, knowing I was in the last minutes of my life. I had abandoned the Catholic faith when I was young, but now at death's door I prayed to the God I had deserted when I embarked on this life of crime. There was no priest available to hear my last confession, so I confessed my sins directly to our lord. I remembered Maralita and how much I loved her, and how she had deceived me. Still, I forgave her, and said a prayer for her soul.

Then the steel door swung open and Hector walked in accompanied by Pasqual.

Time's up. Prepare to die.

~ ~ ~

Pasqual took a position behind my chair. I tried to turn my head to see him, but was restrained by my bounds.

Hector pulled up a chair directly in front of me and sat down. His eyes bore into mine.

"Over the past year I've had two money shipments hijacked from me, both in the States, both when the cars my people were driving were intercepted on the road and the drivers killed. I lost a half-million dollars."

Hector paused and lowered his eyes as if to

commemorate those unhappy days. Not for the drivers. For the money.

"I didn't realize it at the time, but the thief who masterminded those hijacked shipments was Gilberto. Maralita joined him in his insidious efforts when she was released from prison."

"I ..."

Hector held up his hand to stop me. "You will listen and not speak unless I tell you to." He stopped talking for a moment. His jaw muscles rippled.

"Both Gilberto and Maralita tricked you. You were the patsy they needed to setup the ultimate scam. Their intention was to use you to hijack a large shipment that combined two or more collections, kill you and run away with the money. In this case, almost two million dollars. They almost succeeded."

I tried to avoid Hector's eyes, but couldn't.

"Do you recall the older couple who preceded you and Maralita?"

I nodded.

"Gilberto had them killed so Maralita and you could take their place."

I gasped. *What kind of monster kills a sixty-something couple? Was any of the love Maralita professed for me real?*

Hector paused and pulled up his chair even closer to me, his face inches from mine. "Did you witness the execution of Gilberto and Maralita?"

As if he didn't know. I barely managed to nod a yes, the memory of Maralita's horrible death fresh and upsetting. Then a thought intruded: *Hector may not be aware that Maralita and I were planning to rip him off. And since Gilberto and Maralita were dead, along with Ahmed and Doris, Hector would never find out. I still had a chance to get out of this.*

"Gilberto and Maralita almost got away with it, and you allowed it to happen under your nose. That doesn't speak highly of you. Now I have to determine whether or not I should spare your life."

I said nothing. My mouth was so dry I didn't think I could spit.

"Greed. Simple greed." He shook his head. "I don't understand it. I paid all of you well. Gave you steady work ... Well, enough of that." He stopped to gather his thoughts.

"Gilberto and Maralita were responsible for the death of Jennifer Stevens, an invaluable asset to my organization, as well as Ahmed Erkan and his assistant. Another invaluable resource I have used from time to time. They were covering their tracks. No witnesses, nobody to finger them. The murders were committed by Dominic Petiago and Rudy Gambrini, members of the Bombanno family in Philadelphia. I only found out when Joe Bombanno, one of my prime customers, contacted me. He discovered that Petiago and Gambrini were working with Gilberto, with the expectation of being paid a half-million dollars. Needless to say, Joe Bombanno took care of the problem. No more Petiago. No more Gambrini."

Hector moved his chair even closer to mine where our knees were almost touching. "Do you realize the trouble you and Maralita and Gilberto caused me?"

"Yes," I croaked.

"I have to rebuild my USA network. I don't know

who to trust anymore." He sighed. "I don't think I'll ever be able to replace Jennifer Stevens. She was a mole with a perfect cover. Not once did anybody suspect her of working with us. Such a pity."

Hector hugged himself as if to shield his wounded organization from this cruel world. "Did you know the police are looking for you in connection with Jennifer's murder?"

"What!"

"The police traced the Glock 9mm handgun that killed her to the gun seller, its previous owner, in Richmond, Virginia. The police showed him your picture, and the seller identified you. And with your prints on the gun, the police decided to look no further."

"I didn't kill her."

Hector chuckled. "You are naïve, Sam, so very naïve. Gilberto had Jennifer killed with your handgun, the Glock, and planted it at the scene of the crime along with one of your fake driver's license that has your picture on it. Needless to say, it was Maralita who gave the handgun and driver's license to Gilberto."

I did remember giving the Glock to Maralita. Was there no end to her betrayal? More important, why is he telling me this? What else does he want from me?

I heard Pasqual's hoarse breathing behind me. It sent cold shivers through my body. Without another word, Hector rose from his chair and quietly left the room. *It's over now. It's over.* I shut my eyes and said a final prayer.

~ ~ ~

It seemed a lifetime, but minutes later Hector

returned with the two thugs. He sat down in the chair facing me, with the thugs flanking him.

"Untie him," Hector commanded Pasqual.

I couldn't believe it. *Why untie me if you're going to kill me?* Pasqual cut my bonds. I stood on rubbery legs and stretched and massaged my arms, trying to alleviate their soreness.

Hector pointed to the thugs in turn. "This is Pepe and this is Bolino. You already know Pasqual. These men are going to be working with you."

I was stunned. "Working with me? Doing what?"

"I will tell you, but first I want you to understand that you will never be able to return to the States. The police in Memphis, along with the FBI, have declared that you ..." He interrupted himself to open his smart phone and read from an online story in a Memphis newspaper. "Sam O'Hara, an unemployed white-collar worker is wanted for the brutal murder of Jennifer Stevens, a minister of The Church of Our Heavenly Mercy. Police are hunting him nationwide for this heinous crime. His picture, taken when he was in the employ of Bowkart Industries in Atlanta, is shown below. Anybody aware of his whereabouts should report it to their local police department. The FBI has established a hot line for capturing information. Call 1-800-555-1200."

When Hector stopped reading I opened my mouth to raise my objections, but my throat was dry and I had trouble speaking.

"Accept that you can never return home," Hector said. "It is what it is. Accept it and we can move on."

I was in a daze. This was happening too suddenly.

I can't go home anymore!

"You're alive," Hector said, "for two reasons. First, I don't believe you were involved in Gilberto and Maralita's plan to steal my money. The second is that I can use your help in one of my operations."

Thank God, he's not going to kill me. "What kind of help?" I managed to croak out.

"Managerial help. You worked for large companies so you have a basic knowledge of how to run operations efficiently. I'm in need of that expertise now."

Those were approximately the same words I'd heard from the staff at C-Level Careers America, the career marketing firm. They encouraged me to expand my horizons and seek general management work. And now Hector was offering me a managerial job. *It took a drug lord to get me employed gainfully again, and how fucking ironic was that.* I started to titter, then couldn't hold it in any longer, and broke out in a laugh and laughed so hard tears poured down my cheeks.

Hector looked at me in astonishment. As best I could, through bouts of laughter, I explained how I had been unable to land a job in the USA, and that it wasn't until I became a criminal that I received a management offer.

Hector listened, then slowly broke out in a smile while I continued to laugh uncontrollably.

After a few minutes the laughing subsided. Hector leaned forward and tapped my knee. "I have that general management position you want, Sam. One of my operations has not been producing to its potential. There's a lot of demand for the product but their output has plateaued. That's where you come in. We'll see just how good a general manager you are."

"What's the product?"

"Methamphetamine."

TWENTY-FOUR

Hector's drug trade includes production and distribution of cocaine, meth, marijuana and heroin. He distributes and sells his products worldwide. The USA and Europe are his two biggest markets, although his tentacles reach into Turkey, Australia, New Zealand and more recently Russia. It is safe to say that Hector's organization is the largest supplier of drugs on four of the world's seven continents, and most probably in the entire world.

I don't know this for a fact, but I've been led to believe that total sales of the Sinaloa cartel worldwide exceed that of Walmart and Toyota combined, which, if true, would make the Sinaloa cartel the largest privately-held commercial company in the world. Hard to fathom, but even if untrue, you still have to consider the Sinaloa cartel among the world's largest companies. And, just like the world's biggest banks, it is too big to fail. Too many Mexicans and other nationals depend on it for employment. When a company reaches a certain size, such as the Sinaloa cartel, it becomes an institution of the state, which will do anything in its power to keep it alive and flourishing.

There's a reason the Federales focus more on stopping the flow of cocaine and heroin and marijuana. It's because meth generates the fattest profits, and the most profitable drug is protected by both lawful and unlawful entities through payoffs and political pressure. The meth division of the Sinaloa cartel forks over 20 percent of the income it generates to greedy government politicians and law enforcement officers in Mexico and other countries worldwide where the product is marketed. The very same politicians and law enforcement officers who would sell their mothers as street whores to pocket an extra buck, but settle instead for squeezing money from Hector.

~ ~ ~

A few years ago, Hector invested 5.5 million dollars to build an underground meth lab encased in concrete and steel. He purchased the finest equipment needed for meth cooking to produce top-quality, high-potency meth crystals. Add to that the cartel's exceptional distribution skills and superior law enforcement avoidance techniques, and you can appreciate how the drug cartel flourishes.

The problem, as Hector explained it to me, was that the demand for meth had outpaced the ability of the lab to produce enough to satisfy an ever-expanding market.

And that was the heart of my assignment: Apply modern management techniques to supply and meet the explosive demands of the marketplace with high quality methamphetamine.

The meth lab was located in the Lacandona rainforest in the southeastern Mexican state of Chiapas. It's about 70 miles from the Gulf of Mexico, a port through which I passed, along with Pasqual, Pepe and Bolino, on my way to the lab for the first time.

Large portions of this area had been deforested to make way for agriculture and cattle ranches, but enough of the jungle remained to make it difficult for Federales or renegade American DEA agents to locate the meth lab.

This meth lab I manage is the largest of its kind in the USA or Central and South America, to the best my knowledge. It's protected by local police departments that allow it to function unimpeded, and in fact protect it by assuring that its operations are never disturbed by outsiders. A lot of money changes hands to make that happen.

I've been running the meth lab now for five months. When I started, the lab was working one 10.5-hour shift per day. I immediately worked backward in the supply

chain to increase our stock of industrial chemical methylamine, the most important ingredient of the process, along with the dozen other chemicals required, such as acetone and iodine crystals, and lab equipment like reaction vessels, plastic storage containers and large glass beakers.

Lacking the proper quantity of raw material ingredients, the lab had been unable to increase output. It was my purchasing knowledge that allowed me to quickly identify raw material sources, persuade vendors to jack up shipments and negotiate contracts to keep purchasing costs low and shipments to us on-time, a difficult task given that the meth lab is located in a jungle. With enough supplies on hand I was able to double production by placing the lab on two 10.5-hour shifts.

I used Pepe and Bolino to recruit and hire enough reliable employees from the local population to staff the expansion, and the lab's four chemists to train the recruits. Pepe is now in charge of the day shift and Bolino the night shift. Each has responsibility for two chemists and a crew of workers. Pasqual stays on the day shift and is in charge of security.

We effectively doubled gross output and income while keeping costs in line with revenue. I recognized we could probably produce more, but it takes three hours every day to clean the tanks and maintain the equipment. Product purity and quality could easily slip without that necessary attention. So, for right now, production hours are capped at 21 hours a day, seven days a week.

Hector is providing the money to expand our current meth lab production even further. He believes he can sell double the quantity of meth crystal our growth has already produced. We are currently discussing the advantages and disadvantages of either expanding the current lab or building another lab in another part of Mexico. I favor a separate facility. It would protect our goal of an uninterrupted supply of meth to the market in the event of an emergency at our current facility. An emergency such as an unexpected DEA raid or a natural calamity such as an earthquake.

Whatever the outcome, I have engaged a prominent Mexican architect to develop plans for both expansion of our existing facility and a separate plan for building a new meth lab. If Hector's ambitious plans bear fruition, it is possible we will need both. The four chemists we employ will let me know what extra chemicals and equipment will be needed for each alternative. I'm planning on doubling production capacity again within 15 months if all goes according to plan, and it's my job to make sure it does.

I have to admit I enjoy the work. Hell, I *love it.* It keeps me agreeably busy applying a combination of business knowledge and people skills I acquired in corporate America. I know how to motivate workers to pursue common goals mutually beneficial for both company and employee. And I'm learning how to drive production. I'm finding that I'm good at it.

I have an understanding of meth lab metrics and how to apply them to meet high standards, spot opportunities for improvements and correct production and quality problems that interfere with us meeting scheduled weekly shipments.

I also have my hand in the financial side of the business. I personally keep the books, notably pounds of meth shipped, total costs, cost per pound of meth shipped, labor efficiency, product quality, machine uptime and a host of other measurements that help me stay on top of the business.

We cut through nearby jungle for an airstrip, assembled a sheet-metal hanger and own two small single-engine airplanes for shipping our product to various distribution points in Central America and along the southern border of the USA.

I'm anticipating record production for this year and for many years to follow. As long as Hector's salespeople open new markets, and bring new distributors and drug dealers onboard, I vowed to keep meth production current with sales demands, and have done so since my appointment as general manager.

~ ~ ~

Hector bought the nearby hacienda of a retiring farmer and converted it into a private air-conditioned hotel and restaurant for myself, Pasqual, Pepe, Bolino and several meth lab workers who don't live locally and need a place to stay during the week. All of this at no cost to any of us. Little expense is spared. The rooms and suites we occupy beat the standards set by Marriott Hotels for comfort and convenience.

We have an indoor gym and indoor/outdoor pool. What we don't have is a bar because Hector insists that his employees abstain from drinking or taking drugs. Anybody not adhering to the rules is fired and you never hear from them again, and I'm certain everybody knows what "never hear from them again" means.

I don't receive a salary. Hector thinks I might run off if I have a cache of money, and he's not about to let me go. Not after what I've done to professionalize his meth lab operation. I'm much too valuable to him.

Hector pampers me. He allows me to buy anything I want, within reason. For example, I drive a $100,000 supercharged V8 four-wheel-drive Range Rover, a superb vehicle for roaring through unpaved jungle roads, and get an unlimited supply of gasoline from a gas pump at the hotel. I keep garaged a $150,000 Porsche 911 that I take on the road every now and then, but quite honestly, the roads down here are mostly dirt and they turn to mud from frequent rains, so it's not that much fun to drive a sports car without an open asphalt road to test its audacity. Still, it's nice to have and admire.

I also have a roomy seashore bungalow in Pariaso, on the Gulf of Mexico, complements of Hector. I get away from the meth lab about two weekends every month, sit on the beach, dine at fancy restaurants and go night-clubbing. But come Sunday evening around 6:00 p.m. it's back to the hotel at Chiapas in preparation for Monday morning 7:00 a.m. at the meth lab.

The bottom line is that Hector coddles his meth lab employees, especially me, in luxury. He is so generous that employees never want to leave his employ. They can't get a better deal anywhere else in all of Mexico. It contributes to employee retention. That's what I call smart management.

I have a new girlfriend. Her name is Isabel and she works in the hotel and restaurant where I live. She is 20-years-old and quite attached to me. At times I suspect that Hector planted her there to keep me happy. But so what, even if he did, she is a really nice young lady, easy to be around, and needless to say, breathtakingly beautiful. Man does not live by bread alone.

Isabel is teaching me Spanish. I speak it and understand it well enough now to get along in any setting where only Spanish is spoken. I'm not fluent, but I'm getting there. It enables me to better communicate with our meth lab employees, especially Pasqual, Pepe and Bolino.

I don't trust Pasqual. A vivid recollection of him

slicing through Maralita's throat haunts me. I never turn my back on him. I'm sure Hector keeps him around to remind me of my duty to the meth lab. I don't like it, but at least Pasqual obeys my instructions and does a good job securing our meth lab and arranging for transportation of equipment and supplies.

I still think of Maralita from time to time. It's now clear that she and Gilberto planned the two-million-dollar heist right from the get go. She used me to steal the money from Hector. Their intention was to have me take the fall while she and Gilberto bolted and lived happily ever after.

I did love her, and we had a great adventure together. I try to forget how she used me and the memory of how she rushed into Gilberto's arms in Belize. Yet, all in all, I have fond memories of her. And I pray for her soul.

I've returned to the Catholic Church for the first time since I was a teenager. Isabel and I attend services on Wednesday and Sunday and on special occasions such as Easter and Christmas. It feels good to be back in the embrace of the church. It was the missing part of my life.

I realize this sounds hypocritical since I'm in the drug business and my success at doubling meth crystal output damages untold numbers of drug users, but how else can I live with myself?

I'll probably never go back home. How I yearn to see the Atlanta Braves play baseball in the spring, or drink a beer with my wonderful friends at Bowkart and share stories, or see the annual Christmas show at the Fox Theatre in Atlanta, or watch the sun set over Lake Lanier. So many wonderful memories.

Every now and then, especially on evenings when Isabel is visiting her parents in Villamermosa   and I'm alone, I wonder if America will ever be the same for white-collar workers such as in my former life. They're the first group of American workers to hit the street in a downturn, and the most likely never to receive the same amount of wages when they return to work. If they ever return to work. Many, like myself, never do. I don't think my story of chasing the lost American dream is unique.

I follow current events, mainly through online news sources, and I have yet to read about a lessening of the problem. If anything, more and more companies are finding ways to do without their former levels of white-collar employees through corporate mergers, in-house job combinations, demotions from salaried employee to blue collar worker, early retirement and technology improvements. Especially technology improvements. I wish all those unfortunate folks the very best. I sure as hell struck out in the States. Maybe they'll have better luck.

As for me, looks like I'll remain in Mexico.

For the remainder of my life.

ABOUT THE AUTHOR

Zane Smith is a retired company president who has studied white-collar unemployment. He specializes in exposing how white-collar workers lose their jobs and the methods they use to find new employment opportunities, and why most of those attempts are unsuccessful.

After retirement, he worked for a career marketing firm that helps unemployed white-collar workers find jobs, especially those over 50-years-old.

This novel examines the plight of one such white-collar worker.

ABSOLUTELY AMA⚡ING eBOOKS

AbsolutelyAmazingEbooks.com

or AA-eBooks.com

www.ingramcontent.com/pod-product-compliance
Lightning Source LLC
Chambersburg PA
CBHW061454030726
47503CB00005B/1703